Juniors

Published by Merlyn's Pen, Inc.
4 King Street
P.O. Box 1058
East Greenwich, Rhode Island 02818-0964

Printed in the United States of America.

These are works of fiction. All characters and events portrayed in this book are fictional, and any resemblance to real people or incidents is purely coincidental.

Cover design by Alan Greco Design.
Cover illustration by Tim Greene. Copyright ©1995.

Library of Congress Cataloging-in-Publication Data

Juniors : fourteen short stories by eleventh grade writers / edited by
    Kathryn Kulpa.
        p.   cm. -- (The American teen writer series)
    "All of the short stories and essays in this book originally
appeared in Merlyn's Pen: The national magazines of student
writing"--Acknowledgments.
    Summary: A collection of short stories on various topics, written
by students in the eleventh grade.
    ISBN 1-886427-07-0
    1. Short stories, American. 2. Youths' writings, American.
[1. Short stories.   2. Youths' writings.]   I. Kulpa, Kathryn.
II. Series.
PZ5.J925   1996
[Fic]--dc20   95-33613
                                                      CIP
                                                       AC

99 98 97 96   6 5 4 3 2

Juniors

FOURTEEN SHORT STORIES BY ELEVENTH GRADE WRITERS

Edited by
Kathryn Kulpa

The American Teen Writer Series
Editor: R. James Stahl

Merlyn's Pen, Inc.
East Greenwich, Rhode Island

Acknowledgments

Jo-Ann Langseth, copy editor, and Christine Lord, managing editor, are gratefully acknowledged for their significant work in preparing these manuscripts for original publication in *Merlyn's Pen: The National Magazines of Student Writing*.

The American Teen Writer Series

Young adult literature. What does it mean to you?

Classic titles like *Lord of the Flies* or *Of Mice and Men*—books written by adults, for adult readers, that also are studied extensively in high schools?

Books written for teenagers by adult writers admired by teens—like Gary Paulsen, Norma Klein, Paul Zindel?

Shelves and shelves of popular paperbacks about perfect, untroubled, blemish-free kids?

Titles like *I Was a Teenage Vampire? Lunch Hour of the Living Dead?*

The term "young adult literature" is used to describe a range of exciting literature, but it has never accounted for the stories, poetry, and nonfiction actually written by young adults. African American literature is written by African Americans. Native American stories are penned by Native Americans. The Women's Literature aisle is stocked with books by women. Where are the young adult writers in young adult literature?

Teen authors tell their own stories in *Merlyn's Pen: The National Magazines of Student Writing.* Back in 1985 the magazine began giving young writers a place for their most compelling work. Seeds were planted. Now, the American Teen Writer Series brings us the bountiful, rich fruit of their labors.

Older readers might be tempted to speak of these authors as potential writers, the great talents of tomorrow. We say: Don't. Their talent is alive and present. Their work is here and now.

About the Author Profiles:

The editors of the American Teen Writer Series have decided to reprint the author profiles as they appeared in *Merlyn's Pen* when the authors' works were first published. Our purpose is to reflect the writers' school backgrounds and interests at the time they wrote these stories.

Contents

What would she be without them?

Family

by KATE WILKINSON

Ding! Dong!

Jonson Delilah Hill, aged thirteen years, shoved the roast beef into the oven and ran to the front hall. She pulled open the door. The Perfect Suburban Family was standing on the porch of the Hill's dilapidated country home. Aunt Tilly in a lavender suit, understated makeup, and artfully tossed blonde hair. Uncle Greg in shades, lightweight button-down shirt, and khaki pants. Little Cousin Steffie in a pink knit dress and white sandals. All three smiled with Christian forgiveness at Jonson's oversized men's floral shirt, blue jeans, and canvas shoes. Jonson felt a nervous breakdown coming on. She forced a smile.

"Hi, Aunt Tilly! Uncle Greg! Steffie! It's so good to see you. Come put your things in the guest room. No, Grannie won't be here till later. Grandpa George is down at the creek fishing, I think. Mom's in the city working. She should be here soon."

Jonson helped Tilly and Steffie and Greg unload their belongings and invited them to the kitchen for a cold drink. She glanced cautiously out the sink window into the backyard. Grandpa George and his 35-year-old Russian lover, Mikhail, seemed content with their fishing. Jonson made a wishful incantation to keep them there as long as possible. This Memorial Day family reunion would have been a disaster even without them. Jonson checked the clock and wondered if her mother, or Martha as she preferred, really was coming home. As far as Jonson knew, Martha had never held a real job, but currently she was a priestess at the Urban Witches' Covenant Revival Center. Three days ago a novice had phoned to say that the Exalted Mother Martha had gone into a religious trance.

"Please, Mom, break the trance for supper, please," prayed Jonson while she rescued a plate of cream puffs from Steffie. Jonson poured four glasses of iced tea and brought them to the kitchen table.

"Here you go," she said. "Uncle Greg. Aunt Tilly. Here Steffie, careful, don't spill."

Jonson sat down with the others.

"So how was your trip?"

"Just fine, honey, just fine," answered Tilly. "It was really the most lovely drive up here. The flowers were in bloom everywhere. Weren't they lovely, Greg?"

"Yep. They sure were, sure were," said Uncle Greg as he stirred three teaspoons of sugar into his tea.

"So how's the school year been, dear?" asked Tilly in Good Aunt fashion.

"Pretty good," said Jonson. "I'm doing well in all of my classes, especially social studies. I had some trouble with pre-algebra, but Mikhail helped me through that."

Aunt Tilly's pinned-up smile fell.

"Oh, how nice," she said. Uncle Greg coughed nervously, and Steffie blew bubbles into her iced tea. Jonson was immediately lost in a huge drink. She mentally kicked herself for saying the taboo name. The family had nearly split when Grannie Em had moved out of the house thirteen years ago and Martha and her baby daughter had moved in. However, when 22-year-old defector Mikhail Yakov took up residence, the family entered chaos. As far as Jonson could tell from Memorial Day reunions, it had never exited. She gulped down the last of her tea and turned to Steffie.

"So what have you been up to, Stef?" she asked politely.

"I've been in the first grade mostly. Except when I poured glue on the teacher's chair. Then I was in the principal's office for almost three days it seemed like."

Everyone laughed, grateful for the relief from the tension. Jonson left the group to tend to supper, and Aunt Tilly got up to help. Uncle Greg found some crayons and colored with Steffie. An hour later the doorbell rang again.

Jonson called "I'll get it" to Aunt Tilly, who was using a food processor she had apparently brought with her, and ran to the door. Jonson crossed her fingers for Martha, but instead was greeted by a distinguished lady in her fifties. Grannie Em was neatly dressed in gray slacks, a white blouse, and a black blazer; she carried a modern-looking black purse with silver clasps. Jonson groaned inwardly. Grannie was everything Jonson wasn't.

"Good afternoon, Jonson Delilah," said Grannie

Em crisply. "Is that Tilly and the others I hear back there?"

"Um, yes, Grannie," said Jonson, but Emily Hill was already clicking her high heels down the hallway. Jonson sighed. She couldn't remember a time when it wasn't impossible to say even hello to Grannie. Jonson knew that Aunt Tilly and Grannie together were more than she could stand at the moment. She ran upstairs to her mother's bedroom and searched the address book. She didn't find what she was looking for, so she pulled the phone up onto the bed and sat with it. She dialed the operator.

"Hello? Yes. I need a number for the Urban Witches' Covenant Revival Center in downtown . . . OK, 613-5948. Thanks."

Jonson dialed the number and waited six rings before a young, vague voice answered.

"Hi, I'm Exalted Mother Martha's daughter. I was wondering if she's come out of trance yet? Yes, I know we're all spiritual daughters of the Exalted Mother, but I'm her *real* daughter! Is she out of the trance yet? Oh, thank goodness! Can I talk to her?"

Jonson stood up and did a dance on her mother's bed while she waited for the young witch to get Martha.

"Hello? Martha? Oh, I am so glad to hear your voice. Listen. You've got to get here. Uncle Greg and Aunt Tilly and Steffie and Grannie Em are here. Yeah, Mom, yes I know they aren't blessed by the wisdom of the Goddess Gaia. They aren't blessed by any wisdom at all, but you have to get home. OK. Good. And Martha! Martha! Please dress normal. Normal? Well, Mom, just no tie-dyed robes, all right? Bye."

Jonson set down the phone. "Please, Goddess Gaia,"

she whispered. "You've taught the Exalted Mother Martha wisdom; now could you please teach her some common sense?"

Jonson looked at her mother's bedroom clock. It was 5:36. Martha would be home by 6:00. The roast would be done by 6:45. If she could just keep Grandpa George and Mikhail out of the house until the Exalted Mother arrived, there would be only 45 minutes of all-out family warfare before supper. Jonson raced down the stairs, out the front door, and around the house to the backyard. She caught her breath by the garden before walking down to the creek where Grandpa and Mikhail were talking and fishing.

"Hi, Grandpa George. Hi, Mikhail. Caught anything yet?"

Grandpa laughed. "Nothing big enough to keep. Lots of five-inchers, though."

Mikhail sighed dramatically.

"I," he said, "I have caught nothing. I never catch anything. These American fishes are prejudiced, I think."

Jonson sat down on the bank. "Did you catch very many in Russia?"

Mikhail faked a sob. "No! Never."

All three broke up laughing. Grandpa cast his line into the deep hole near the raspberry bush.

"I suppose everyone is here now?" he said.

"Everyone except for Martha. She came out of her trance, though. Should be home by six."

Grandpa George shook his head slowly.

"I love your mother dearly," he said, "but you do realize that she is completely crazy."

"Yeah," said Jonson. She threw a pebble into the creek. "I realize it. I told her to dress normal. I hope she does. Anyway, supper won't be ready until 6:45 or thereabouts, so I was thinking, if you guys stayed here till Martha shows up . . ."

Mikhail interrupted, saying, "Trying to keep everyone from breaking all of the dishes in the house and the lamps, too?"

Jonson giggled. "Precisely."

She climbed up from her seat on the bank. Grandpa George reeled in and cast again.

"I think we can manage that, Jonson." He looked up at Mikhail, who nodded in agreement.

"Thanks, Grandpa. Bye. See you, Mikhail." Jonson walked back to the house.

Mission accomplished, she thought. *Now all I've got to do is put up with Aunt Tilly and Grannie Em for a little while, and Martha will be here in a half-hour, and dinner will need looking after up till then* . . . Jonson opened the screen door into the kitchen.

"Fishing?" asked Grannie sarcastically. She was grating cheese over some sort of casserole. Jonson didn't answer. Instead, she opened the oven and spooned juices over the roast. She peeled potatoes silently while Grannie Em and Aunt Tilly gossiped. Uncle Greg was in the living room now, watching the news on television. Steffie was underfoot. Jonson felt that she was managing well until Grannie Em turned to her and asked, "I hear you took part in some sort of coming-of-age ceremony in February. I'd like to know more about it."

Jonson blushed. She was not going to tell Grannie Em and Aunt Tilly about the Urban Witches' ceremonial dance for young girls who have just had their first period.

"It was at our church. Just like a First Communion, really," Jonson lied, and went back to her potatoes. She switched to carrots and the three were silent. Steffie wandered out the back door. At 6:07 the crunch of an old station wagon rolling up the gravel driveway reached them. Aunt Tilly looked up.

"That's Martha, I imagine," she said wearily. "Will you fetch Steffie, Jonson dear? I believe she's playing out back."

"Sure," said Jonson. She didn't want to witness the first greetings anyway. Jonson opened the screen door and walked slowly to Stef, who was playing at the far corner of the yard near the old pine. Grandpa and Mikhail had already left the creek and were meeting Martha at her car. Jonson noticed with satisfaction that the Exalted Mother Martha was dressed comparatively tamely in a black skirt, shapeless crimson blouse, various crystals, and leather sandals. Jonson sat down under the tree next to Steffie.

"Hi, Stef. What're you doing?"

The first low sounds of quarreling were issuing from the house. Martha and Mikhail's presence always lit the fire.

"I'm making a little fort, see?" Steffie showed Jonson her carefully arranged dirt, twigs, and pine cones. Jonson nodded enthusiastically.

"That's neat," she said. "What if we made a little road over here?" Jonson and Steffie played for fifteen or twenty minutes while the low quarreling sounds rose to the volume of a hurricane. At the cry of "Merciful Goddess Gaia, Save Her Untaught Soul!" and a following "For the Love of Jesus Christ!" Jonson stood up and helped Steffie to her feet.

"I guess we'd better go in and see what's going on," she sighed.

Steffie ran up to the house. Seeing the grownups fight was a great source of entertainment. Much better than sticks and dirt. Jonson followed reluctantly. She went through the kitchen and stood in the hallway. She was roughly in the eye of the storm. Grandpa George and Grannie Em were shouting at one another at the front door.

Probably just started fighting there and never bothered to move, thought Jonson. She caught snatches of "It's absolutely sickening! Keeping our disaster of a daughter here in the house is bad enough. But that horrid boy-creature? What do you think people think?" and "I've been telling you for thirteen years, Emily! We're in love! And that's more than I ever could have said for you and me."

Martha and Aunt Tilly were upstairs somewhere. Aunt Tilly's high, indignant voice carried downstairs.

"But, Martha! You're raising the girl as a heathen. Why, anyone could tell by looking at her that she's an atheist!"

Martha's best priestess tone rang back. "My daughter and I are both blessed by the Goddess Gaia."

Jonson shook her head sadly. Gaia, Buddha, Ra . . . Martha had tried almost every religion known to man. Jonson listened for Uncle Greg and Mikhail. They were in the living room and were much calmer than the others. So far as Jonson could tell, they were discussing foreign trade policies.

Martha, Aunt Tilly, Grandpa, and Grannie became more and more heated.

Oh, what am I going to do? thought Jonson over

and over. *They have to stop for supper. They have to.*

Steffie rushed down the stairs giggling.

"Jonson! Jonson! Come see!" shouted Steffie, jumping up and down. "Auntie Martha and Mommy are fighting. Come see!"

Jonson grabbed hold of Steffie and made her stand still.

"Oh, what am I going to do?!" she cried aloud. The scent of burning meat made up her mind for her. Jonson dragged Steffie into the kitchen and sat her down at the table. She turned off the oven and removed the roast. It was not badly burnt. Jonson placed the roast on the table along with the other food. She began rummaging in the pantry. When she found the old cymbals left over from her brief band days, she ran into the hall with them. Martha, Aunt Tilly, Grandpa, and Grannie were still shouting. Mikhail and Uncle Greg were talking loudly now. Jonson closed her eyes and, with a cymbal in each hand, spread her arms wide.

CRASH!

"Everybody! Suppertime!!!"

The house was silent. Jonson carried the cymbals back into the kitchen and set them on the counter. She sat at the head of the table. Steffie stared at her in awe.

"That was loud," she whispered.

One by one the grownups filed in. Uncle Greg first, looking embarrassed, then Mikhail, trying to keep from laughing. Grannie Em marched in furiously, patting down her hair and striving to regain dignity. Grandpa George came behind, grinning. Aunt Tilly entered with her suburban housewife face only slightly flushed and Martha followed last, the very picture of controlled holy rage. Everyone sat.

"Um . . . Would you like to say grace, Jonson?" suggested Aunt Tilly timidly. Jonson nodded. Everyone bowed his or her head except for Martha.

"Dear God," started Jonson. Martha glared wrathfully across the table. Jonson continued smoothly, "and Spirit of the Great Goddess Gaia, we thank you." Jonson paused and smiled happily around the table.

"We thank you for family."

ABOUT THE AUTHOR

Kate Wilkinson is a student at the Interlochen Arts Academy in Interlochen, Michigan, and a native of Sheridan, Montana. Majoring in creative writing at Interlochen, she also enjoys playing the violin, hiking, swimming, and cartooning.

Sometimes honesty can end a friendship.
Sometimes it can make it stronger.

Jase's Gift

by Ashley Bourne

The summer I turned sixteen came with balloons and roses from my friends, a beat-up black Jeep from my parents, and a half-empty pack of cigarettes from my cousin Jase.

They weren't for me to smoke; it was Jase's last pack. He gave the rest to me after he decided to quit. The Jeep has long since been scrapped, the balloons deflated, and the roses lay dead and pressed between the pages of my dictionary. But I keep that dusty pack of Camels in my dresser drawer and remember that summer.

Jase was eighteen when he came that June; his mother had just died. I never knew their family very well because they lived in Cassidy, an eight-hour drive from our house. I remember him at the funeral: he had shaggy blond hair to his shoulders and dark circles under his eyes. I was staring at his black suit—it looked severely starched and a year's growth too small.

My mother told me then that he was going to stay with us for the summer.

"Just until things get straightened out. The poor boy, with his mother dying so suddenly, your Uncle Neil just can't take care of all the kids until some, ah, arrangements are made. It's just for the summer, hon." With that, she patted my shoulder absently and moved away to speak to my father.

I felt betrayed. I had always been an only child, and now I had to share my house—for the whole summer—with a cousin I had seen only on Christmas, and even then we spoke little.

Later, as I was leaving, I saw him in back of the funeral home, alone. I had come out before my parents, and I was heading for the car when I saw the lean figure out of the corner of my eye. I squinted at him briefly; he was right in front of the sun. He was smoking, and all of a sudden I felt sorry for him. I wasn't sure why, and it troubled me for several days.

Jase arrived the weekend after we got out of school. My mother asked me to get his bed ready after dinner, so I went upstairs and tiptoed into his room while he was watching television. He walked in as I was putting on the pillowcases. He looked startled.

"Hi. I was just, ah, changing the sheets."

"Oh, OK." We fell silent again. I felt like I needed to say something.

"I'm really sorry about your mom." I regretted it the instant it was out of my mouth, and my awkward expression of sympathy made him uncomfortable.

"Yeah, well . . ." But he never finished, and his eyes never left the window.

"Goodnight," I said and left him alone with his thoughts.

He remained sullen and quiet for the first few weeks. We barely spoke; I felt awkward because I didn't know what to say, and I think he felt edgy anyway. He liked to be by himself, and I wasn't really surprised when I found him one day in the woods behind our house, sitting at the base of my favorite tree. It was always the place I came to be by myself and think. He was smoking, eyes half-closed and barefoot. He turned his head warily toward me.

"Hi," I said. My smile faded as he just looked through me.

"Hey," he answered, and turned back to whatever he had been staring at. I sat down near him. I had no idea what to say.

"So, um . . . how are you doing . . . here, I mean? What do you think of the town and all?" I was trying, but I had no clue as to what was going on in his mind.

"It's OK, I guess. Not much to do." He took another drag on his cigarette and blew out a toxic cloud of smoke.

"Can you do rings?" I asked.

"Nope," he answered. We sat in silence a minute before he spoke again, hesitantly. "I can blow smoke out of my nose, though." And he did. I smiled.

The smoke was starting to drift my way. It stung my eyes a little, and I coughed when it curled up my nose. He gave me an appraising look.

"Want to try one?" he asked, holding the glowing stick out to me. Tempted, I looked at it for a second, then snatched it up and put it to my lips. I drew the smoke into my mouth and held it there, rolling my eyes toward him for directions.

"OK, inhale it now," he said. I pulled the thickness into my lungs and I felt it burning my throat and lighting up my insides until I knew they must be glowing like the tip of his Camel. It hurt, and I parted my lips to exhale. A tumult of angry smoke poured out of my mouth—much more than went in, I'm sure—and my tongue tasted like singed tobacco. I handed him the cigarette back.

"That's pretty good. You didn't even cough," he said. I turned away and spat to get the nasty, burnt taste out of my mouth. It didn't help.

"What?" he asked.

"That tastes awful. You should quit, you know."

"Nah. I've been smoking too long," he said in a lofty tone.

"How long?"

He didn't answer immediately; he looked away.

"Two years," he said, darting his blue eyes at me to see if I believed him.

"Oh," I said.

We sat in silence until I looked at my watch. It was almost two o'clock. I was meeting my friends at the pool, so I got up to leave. He watched me. I knew I should invite him to go, but I didn't really want him to come along. I didn't think he'd enjoy himself and I'd end up feeling guilty being with my friends, so I'd have to go and sit with him and try to be friendly while all my friends had a wonderful time. I asked anyway. I felt him studying me with those sharp eyes.

"Nah. I don't feel like it," he answered, so I turned to go, relieved, and left him with a hasty "OK, bye."

Still, I couldn't enjoy myself at the pool for thinking about Jase alone in the woods. I ended up sitting alone at the edge of the pool anyway, wondering if he didn't like me.

And so it went for several more weeks; I would find Jase at the base of the tree, or sometimes in it, but always smoking and always staring off into the distance. I would sit down, or sometimes climb up into the giant branches, and we would talk a little, or just sit and enjoy the quiet.

He asked me to drive him to 7-Eleven for cigarettes sometimes. I had my learner's permit, and he was eighteen, so my parents let us drive to the store alone for practice before I got my license. Little did they know . . .

I actually started to get to know him, my cousin who smoked, who liked to read Kerouac and Jack London, who liked dogs not cats, whose favorite color was dark green, and who knew just about all there was to know when it came to fishing. And then one day, he wasn't the stranger who had come to stay with us for the summer; he was my cousin Jase. I even let him read my stories.

"These are good," he said. Coming from him, I knew it was a compliment. He was very interested in my writing; he even helped me revise my stories. He was becoming a friend.

But I didn't like driving him to get cigarettes anymore. At first, I thought it was great that he trusted me. We had a secret, and the quick trips to 7-Eleven and going home the long way so he could finish a smoke were fun. But every night, I lay awake and heard the dry cough that plagued him. It was nothing serious, or so he claimed; it only lasted a few minutes.

Still, I felt like it was partly my fault. I felt guilty. So I stopped driving him to buy cigarettes. I knew my parents wouldn't buy him his Camels, and our house was ten miles from the 7-Eleven; I didn't think he'd want to walk that far.

"C'mon. Let's go to the store real fast, OK?" he asked.

"You just bought a pack the other day. Aren't you going through them pretty fast?"

"What's it to you?" His eyes turned wary, and his voice lost the friendly edge I had become used to hearing.

"Well, it's just, you smoke a lot and I feel bad because I know . . ."

"You know what? That your parents wouldn't want me to have them? That my father wouldn't want me to smoke? That you might get in trouble?" He tried to sound nasty, but I think he was mostly shocked; he looked like he'd been double-crossed.

"They'll kill you," I said, feeling like a self-righteous pamphlet—or my mother. "Lung cancer—I don't feel like helping you ruin your lungs. You've been coughing more since you've been here." I tried to explain. His eyes blazed and his face wore a half-amazed, half-betrayed look. I suppose he couldn't believe that I, his only friend here, had refused to support him. He just walked off.

When I went for dinner, my parents asked where Jase was. I said I thought he was in his room, which was true. I thought he'd just gone inside after our argument.

It started to rain halfway through my second slice of pizza. By the time I finished off my Dr. Pepper, thunder crashed and lightning spliced the darkened sky outside. During dessert, the rain really began to pound. My parents had just stepped into the den when the door opened. I looked up from loading the dishwasher. Jase walked in.

He was soaking wet; his clothes were plastered to his body and his hair hung in wet strands as water rolled off his face. Darting his eyes quickly around the room to make sure my parents were not there, he pulled a wet, slightly crumpled pack of Camels triumphantly from the pocket of his jeans. Then he went up to his room. I followed the wet tracks upstairs and was about to knock on the door when I heard him cough and I lost my courage. I tiptoed down the hall to my room.

We didn't speak much for the next week. It wasn't just the smoking that bothered me, it was that he didn't fit into my carefully structured world. I had gotten to know him, but I wasn't sure if I liked everything I knew.

My birthday was a sunny day near the end of August. Jase was leaving for home in a few days. My friends had taken me out all day, first shopping, then to dinner and a late movie. When I walked into the house, it was dark and absorbed in sleep and silence. I crept up to my room. I noticed a small, wrapped package on my dresser. I picked it up gently and peeled off the crumpled wrapping paper. It was a half-empty pack of Camels. The wrapper was water-stained, and there was a note folded between the cigarettes.

Sorry, no money.
Happy Birthday.

These were more trouble than they're worth.
I quit. J.

I felt the smile bursting out on my face. The next morning, Jase had packed his things. I didn't get a chance to talk to him alone, but I hugged him as we walked out to the car. While my parents were talking to Uncle Neil, Jase asked me quietly if I had gotten his present. I smiled, and said I liked that one the best of all.

"You know," he started, "I'd only smoked for a few months. Not really that long," he confessed.

"I knew it all along."

"Yeah, I'll bet!" he laughed as he got into the car.

"Come see us at Christmas!" I called just before they pulled away. Jase waved, and I watched their car as it turned out of our driveway and rolled out of sight.

About the Author

Ashley Bourne lives in Fredericksburg, Virginia, and wrote this story as a student at Stafford Senior High School in Stafford. Editor of her school newspaper, the Stafford Indian Smokesignal, *she has won several awards for her fiction and poetry. Her other interests include horseback riding, filmmaking, and history.*

Two rival elk face each other in battle—but an even
deadlier enemy is watching . . .

Showdown

by ETHAN CAMPBELL

September. Brilliant red and yellow leaves coated
the mountainside in the Colorado sunshine.
Skinny, barren branches of aspen poked out, covering the hilltops with shades of gray. Some dead brown
leaves still clung resolutely to the lower sheltered
branches.

The land was dry. Most of the underbrush had died
long ago and shriveled up, making it brittle and crunchy
underfoot. The slightest movement from any creature
great or small, even from the tiny ground squirrels,
made loud crackles and snaps.

Birds flitted about from tree to tree, chirping, call-
ing each other to gather for the long trip south. Mice
and squirrels scurried along the ground, searching for
nuts and bits of food to store in their burrows for the
next few months. A big brown rattlesnake slithered
underneath a rock, to the warmth and comfort of the
moss and rotted material there. All around, animals

were preparing themselves for the White Death that would soon come in thick clouds over the mountaintops.

A twig snapped. A dried leaf crackled. Slowly and carefully, Ki stepped into the forest clearing.

He was a majestic bull elk, fully grown, and towered like a king over the lesser forest creatures. He must have weighed better than eight hundred pounds, and rippling muscles stood out on the brown coat of his legs and shoulders. Six antlers jutted out proudly on either side of his head.

Ki tilted his head back and bugled, long and full of power. The cry cut through the clear mountain air and echoed off the cliffs and peaks. It was a triumphant bugle. He was free: free to roam, free to run, free to do anything he pleased. And soon another victory would be his. Ki relished the thought of it.

He kept his head tilted back, to keep his antlers from getting tangled in the brush, and charged ahead. His hooves pounded the soft ground, and leaves flew in every direction.

Ki kept running through the aspen, until suddenly the ground beneath him became hard. His hooves clicked and clacked against the black, smelly surface. Manrock, the animals called it. Here he stopped and dropped his head back down. Off in the distance, he heard a low rumbling.

Ki sniffed at the air. His sense of smell was not incredibly acute, but he knew the scent of man well. Man had been here, and with Man come . . . *Aargh!* Ki jumped to the side of the road as the Metalbeast roared past. He felt a cool blast of air hit him, and he dashed into the woods. That had been close. His heart was pounding rapidly.

Yes. With Man come Metalbeasts, he thought. *And Thundersticks.*

These were not things to worry about, though. Man would not get in his way. Very soon he would win his victory. He knew. He could feel it in his bones. Ki tilted his head back and kept moving. He had more pressing business to attend to.

"Awww, c'mon, Dad! Couldn't you have shot him?! He was a six-pointer, for cryin' out loud! We just about hit him with the pickup!"

Mike didn't even bother to look down at his teenage son, Cory. "Of course not. Elk season doesn't start until tomorrow. You ought to know that."

Cory gave him a dumb look. "So, uh, what's your point? We could have shot him, punched in tomorrow's date on the tag, and turned him in in the morning. The warden would never have known."

Mike decided to humor him. "Yeah, I guess you're right. Sorry I didn't think of that."

"If we see another one, will you shoot it?"

"Sure. You pay the five-hundred-dollar fine."

Cory smiled. "Just kidding, Dad."

Ki, tired from his long run, slowed to a walk. He continued to sniff the air, and constantly searched for tracks in the dirt.

Ki pricked up his ears. Ah, here it was. The scent was old, perhaps a couple of sunrises, but his opponent had been here, no doubt.

His opponent in this case was Tak, a bull elk nearly three years older than he, and many times stronger. Tak weighed as much as a bull moose, and sported seven unbroken antlers, a sign of great power. At the shoulder, he stood taller than most Metalbeasts, and his explosive strength was second to none. Other bulls respected him and kept their distance. Tak had a temper and loved to fight.

Ki sniffed again, and stifled his terrified shudder. The scent was unmistakable.

He smelled something else, too. A familiar odor . . .

Lioni! The realization hit him so suddenly, he nearly fell over. Lioni had been here also! Oh, how the smell of her brought back wonderful memories: memories of a beautiful cow elk, young and energetic. And free.

Alas, Lioni was not free now, Ki thought sadly.

He found himself remembering back to the days when he and Lioni were young. They had grown up together, by each other's sides, practically. Their mothers had traveled in the same herd.

Ki remembered fondly how they had often romped and played together in the tall mountain grass. How they had chased after the squirrels and tried to talk to the birds. How they had rolled around together innocently, kicked their hooves in the air and teased each other.

She had been lovely, her young coat a dark velvet. Her blue eyes were bright, full of life.

More than once, Ki had playfully butted Lioni's head, a natural instinct for a young bull. He had not understood why she didn't fight back, or known that she was destined never to have antlers. Neither had he understood why she was so beautiful to him compared to the other young bulls, nor why he was attracted to her. All he knew was that he liked to be with her, and couldn't help staring at her as she pranced in the distance.

Such sweet memories as these flooded his head like a ray of sunshine as he smelled her scent. But these were darkened by a thundercloud of bad memories.

By the time they were each yearlings, Ki had grown two spike antlers on the top of his head, and he more fully understood the ways of nature. That autumn, he planned to take Lioni as his mate. Early in the morning, on a clear September day such as this, he had let out a long, triumphant bugle on a hillside, announcing to the world his decision.

Suddenly, Tak had been there, snorting, pawing the ground, challenging him, full of fight.

Being a spike, Ki could do nothing but turn tail and run, and that was exactly what he had done. He had watched helplessly as Tak had taken Lioni, taken her away, taken her far, far away . . .

That had been three years ago. Ki had not seen Lioni once since the fateful day Tak had defeated him. In fact, this was the first time he had even smelled her scent.

But all of that was about to change.

Lioni had been with Tak for three years and still no calf ran by her side, or so his elk and deer friends had told him. Ki smiled. Ha! So the mighty Tak was not so mighty as he seemed!

Now, for some reason unknown to Ki, Tak had decided to show his face in these parts again. That had been a mistake, Ki thought angrily. His last mistake.

Ki shook his head violently and felt the gigantic

span of his rack swing back and forth. He was ready for Tak this time. The other bull elk might still be bigger than he, but Ki had more determination. This would probably be his last chance to take back Lioni as his mate. His last chance at revenge.

He put his nose to the ground and followed the scent to where it was strongest. Ki looked up. He would have to run all night to catch them.

In the sky, a huge gray cloud loomed threateningly, casting a chill over the countryside. Birds stopped their chirping and flew in the other direction. Squirrels scurried into their holes. That night, though he barely noticed in the heat of his run, it snowed enough to cover his hooves.

The next morning, Mike was out of bed and fixing pancakes for breakfast at six o'clock.

Cory sat up in bed and rubbed the sleep from his eyes. "Awww, Dad, couldn't we have parked the camper somewhere besides on a hill? I have a roaring headache. All the blood rushed to my head."

Mike rolled his eyes. "I told you already, the only flat areas are farther down the mountain. The elk won't be there this early in the fall. We have to stay up as high as we can. Next time, sleep with your head on the uphill side."

Cory grumbled and swung his legs over the side. He bent over to pick up his shoes and started putting them on. "I can't even sit straight, for Pete's sake. Everything feels crooked."

"Quit complaining. We're going to get an elk today. I can feel it in my bones." Mike poured batter into the pan and watched it roll toward him. "Uhh . . . your pancake might be shaped a little funny."

Cory groaned.

Ki allowed himself a moment's rest as dawn broke in the eastern sky. His back was coated with a fine layer of snow and pine needles. His legs ached and his heart pounded heavily, shaking his entire body. He had been running and walking most of the night.

The scent was much stronger here. Yes, Tak and Lioni were very close.

Lying in the cold grass beneath a large pine tree, Ki was able to collect his thoughts. They were probably bedded down somewhere right now, and would stay there for the remainder of the day. Lioni would be asleep, resting, but Tak . . . Ki wasn't sure. Tak might be sleeping, but surely he would be alert, on guard. He would be alert enough to hear a moderately loud noise.

A loud noise like antlers scraping against tree bark.

Ki looked around at the snow-covered trees and shrubs. He was about three miles from the place animals called the Fighting Ground. The Fighting Ground was a forest clearing where deer and elk gathered to settle their disputes, usually over does or cows. He would go there, Ki decided, and send out his challenge to Tak. He would hear it. Oh yes, Tak would hear it, because he would be listening for it.

Ki rested his aching bones for a little while longer, then finally stood up. He shook the snow off himself, then resumed his journey.

Cory was very cold, and was not underemphasiz-
ing that point to his father. "Why didn't you tell me
it was going to snow up here?"

Mike sighed, and shifted the rifle hanging on his
shoulder. "We're in the mountains of Colorado, Cory.
It'll probably snow up here every night from now until April. Complaining about it doesn't make it any
warmer."

"Yeah, yeah. I'm freezing." It was then that Cory
froze. "Dad. C-come here." He was staring at the ground,
mouth hanging open. "Look at the size of these tracks."

Mike walked over and looked at the spot where
Cory's trembling finger pointed. Several gigantic elk
prints cut through the snow down to the dirt beneath.

"Holy smokin' catfish, Dad! How big do you think
it is? How many points?"

"Hard to tell. Don't know if it was even a bull.
Whatever it was, it was going somewhere in an awful
hurry. The tracks are all in a straight line through these
trees, and they're pretty far apart." Mike crouched
down and touched one of the hoofprints with his finger. "They're pretty fresh, too."

Cory smiled and pulled the .270 rifle from his shoulder. "Let's follow them."

The young elk proceeded with caution as he neared
the clearing. Ki sniffed the air and ground, and kept
a careful eye out for any kind of movement in the
brush. He had heard three Thunderstick noises already
today, and it was only noon.

Ki's head suddenly jerked up, his eyes wide with
fear. That smell! That smell! The Bad Smell. Ki looked

at the barren black skeletons of dead trees around him. Yes, this was the place. The Bad Place.

Memories poured into his head like a waterfall. This was a very Bad Place.

Ki remembered the Hot Running Death that had swept through this place, killing everything in its way. And the smell! The horrible choking smell that made his nostrils burn furiously. Ki remembered how the birds had shrieked in warning, and the small forest animals had screamed in mortal pain. Many had lost their lives in this place. It was a Bad Place, indeed.

His mother had died here. The Hot Running Death had caught them unawares, while they were bedded down and sleeping. They had awakened to the cries of the birds, and with the burning smell clogging their noses and throats.

Ki had run, run as fast as he could—fast for a yearling bull—to escape, and left his mother behind. She couldn't move as quickly with the smell in her nostrils. Eventually, she had fallen down and the Hot Running Death had captured her.

His mother's dying screams echoed in Ki's head now as he sniffed at the stumps poking out of the snowy ground.

A noisy woodpecker pulled Ki back into reality. This was a Bad Place, true, but it held nothing for him now. His destination was the Fighting Ground.

Ki turned toward a blackened stump and relieved himself near it. He took one last glance around for memory's sake, then moved on.

Mike puffed and gasped for breath in the thin mountain air. *It's amazing what adrenaline will do for a per-son*, he thought. Before they had found the elk tracks, Cory had wanted to stop and rest every chance he could get. Now Mike could hardly keep up with him.

The older man slowed to a walk. Cory was stopped several yards ahead, looking at something. "What is it?" Mike called.

"Come and take a look at this, Dad. All of these trees are dead."

Mike caught up to his son and looked around at the wooded valley spread before them. He kicked the snow from the top of a stump. The wood underneath was charred and black. "There's been a forest fire in here. It wasn't very big, from the looks—probably put itself out—but was big enough to kill everything in this valley."

Cory pushed over a log with his foot and uncovered a large antlered skull. "Looks like trees weren't the only things that died in the fire."

Both of them were silent for a long time as they viewed the scene of the tragedy, the terrible death that the flames had left behind.

Finally, Cory broke the silence. "Well, our elk has been through here, all right. He left some droppings by this stump."

Mike studied the droppings, and his voice dropped to a whisper. "These are very fresh. We'd better not talk very much from here on out."

Cory nodded in agreement, and led the way out of the valley.

It was midafternoon when Ki reached the Fighting

Ground. He stepped slowly into the clearing and listened to his footsteps crunching in the snow. There were no other elk or deer here, and nothing stirred. Even the wind seemed to sense Ki's presence and stopped its rustling in the branches.

Ki gazed at his surroundings in wonder. This place never ceased to amaze him. None of the evergreen trees in the area had a complete skin of bark. On the lower levels of all the surrounding trees, the bark was stripped from continual antler rubbing. Although it was covered with snow, Ki also knew that there was no grass on the ground. It had been reduced to dirt from the constant pounding and ripping of hooves.

Ki looked at the sun. It was time. He let out a loud, challenging bugle and, with his head lowered, charged into the nearest pine tree. His antlers hit the wood with a crack, and slivers of bark flew in every direction. Ki shook his head back and forth violently, snorting and grunting and pawing the ground. The loud clattering was heard for several miles throughout the forest.

Before too long, Ki's noisemaking paid off. He stopped his clattering and lifted his shoulders. There was a rustling in the bushes behind him. Ki heard a snort and whirled.

Standing in the forest clearing was a medium-sized, young bull elk with a squarish nose. Dol. Ki drooped his shoulders and let down his guard. Dol was a friend.

I see you are in a fighting mood, Dol snorted. *Do you wish to challenge me? I am ready for a showdown.*

Ki shook his head. *No, my little friend. I have no wish to duel with you. I have a larger opponent in mind.*

Who might that be?

Ki was silent.

Tak?

Ki looked down at his hooves.

You are a fool, my friend. It is not my place, however, to tell you who to fight or not fight. You will choose what you think is best for yourself. With that, Dol bounded away.

Ki watched him go with resignation. If only Dol could fight with him, then perhaps things would be all right. Dol, one of his closest friends, had called him a fool. He might have a point.

Doubts crept into Ki's mind. Did he really stand a chance against a bull as powerful as Tak? Was Lioni really worth the risk?

Suddenly, there was another grunt behind him in the brush. As Ki turned, seven huge pointed antlers slammed into his head full force, throwing him off balance. Ki tumbled to the ground, landing on his side with a thud as a huge black form rushed past him. He shook his head to clear it from the blow. When Ki looked up, he saw him.

Tak was standing over Ki, a towering mass of solid muscle. Steam rolled off his back and poured out of his mouth. His red eyes flared in anger, and his face wrinkled with hatred.

When I heard your challenge, I ran here as fast as I could. Get up! Now you will be defeated!

Ki kicked his legs and struggled to his feet. The instant he was up, Tak charged again. Ki sidestepped and sent him skidding into a grove of saplings.

Taking me is not going to be as easy as it was last time, Tak. You're going to have to fight for all you're worth.

Tak pulled himself free from the branches and stepped into the clearing again. Now the two elk were facing each other, with about three yards between them. For several revolutions they paced in circles, each judging the distance to the other and preparing to lunge.

Finally, Ki let out a cry and charged. Tak crouched to meet the blow and lowered his head. Their antlers crashed together in midair and locked. Tak swung his massive body to the right and threw Ki to the side easily.

Ki staggered and stumbled, but managed to keep his feet, and swung around to meet Tak a second time. Although he couldn't see his head, Ki knew that one of his antlers had been broken in the assault.

Ha! You look like a lopsided aspen tree! Tak sneered.

His anger at the boiling point, Ki flew at Tak with renewed fury. Tak once again lowered his head, but Ki kept his head high. The sharp point of the broken antler drove into Tak's upper flank and pierced the hide.

Tak cried out in pain as he stepped back and gave him an astonished look.

Ki smiled maliciously. *You ought to have known I'd fight dirty, old friend.*

Now it was Tak's turn to charge. He came furiously with a growl, and plowed into Ki's broken rack with every bit of his tremendous weight. Ki stood his ground and kept his head low, but the charge was too much for him. He was swept off his feet and flew backwards into the side of a pine tree.

With his momentum, Tak moved forward and planted a sharp hoof into Ki's upturned belly. Ki writhed in pain, and fought to regain his footing.

Get up! I want you to see me coming!

Ki rolled over slowly and started to get up. Tak would not attack him on the ground.

From the corner of his eye, Ki spotted movement on the edge of the clearing . . . two figures, moving stealthily. Although he was colorblind and could not see the blaze orange of their jackets, Ki knew what those figures were.

Ki climbed cautiously to his feet. Tak rushed at him but Ki sidestepped, keeping the other bull between himself and the men. Tak gave him a frustrated look and rushed again, but Ki trotted quickly to the side, making sure that Tak was still blocking the line of fire.

You are running from me! Tak laughed. *Are you giving up?*

Tak charged one last time, putting forth one final blast of energy in an attempt to defeat the younger bull. Ki put his head low and met Tak's charge with a clash of antlers.

Both of them stood with their horns interlocked, staring at each other, hot breath mingling in labored bursts. Tak's features were twisted into a maniacal, victorious smile, but Ki's face was solemn.

Now, my friend, you will die. I will have my revenge.

A loud *crack* broke the stillness in the clearing. Tak jumped and pain flashed through his eyes. Ki worked his antlers free and drew back. Tak dropped to his knees. His breath came in ragged gasps as he stared at Ki in shock and disbelief.

You . . . you . . . coward. You knew . . . you . . . knew! You COWARD!

Tak coughed suddenly and blood spilled out of his mouth.

Coward . . .

His mouth clamped shut and he fell onto his side. His eyes took on a glassy appearance as his head slipped to the ground.

Ki took another step back, transfixed by the scene he had just witnessed. The young bull took one last look, then turned and ran for his life.

"I got him!" Cory shrieked with excitement. "Did you see that, Dad? I got him!"

Mike put his .270 to his shoulder and squeezed off two more rounds, but the fleeing bull didn't flinch. "Ah, shoot! My gun must be firing low."

Cory leaped over the snowbanks toward the fallen elk. He knelt down beside the animal and surveyed its wound. "Straight through the chest. I can't believe it."

Mike jogged up behind him and whistled. "Nice shot, kid."

"Thanks. The stupid elk were too busy fighting to see us sneaking up." Cory scratched his chin thoughtfully. "I wonder what they were fighting about."

Mike shrugged. "Probably some girl."

Ki kept running. His stomach roared with pain where Tak had kicked him, and his head ached from repeated blows. Blindly, he kept running, through the forest, over snowbanks, through tangled underbrush, into an open field.

Suddenly, Lioni was by his side, nuzzling up to his

neck with her nose, rubbing herself against his sweat-soaked body. Ki slowed to a trot as Lioni licked his face and ears. His heart leapt for joy and felt like it was going to explode.

Lioni gestured with her head. *Come with me. I know a place where we will be safe.*

Ki followed obediently, letting her lead the way. At the top of the nearest hill, he stopped to bugle one last time. Now they were both free. As he bugled, long and full of triumph and excitement, Ki reflected on Tak's parting words.

Sure, he was a coward. Who wasn't? At least he had been smart enough not to let that fact defeat him.

Ki let his bugle trail off on a mellow, almost mournful note, then returned to Lioni, his mate. She rubbed her nose against his and smiled.

Everything was going to be all right now.

"All right. Let's hurry up and get this thing out of here," Cory said as he looked at the thousand-pound carcass at his feet. "I'm starting to get cold. And my feet are wet. And my shoulder is sore from carrying this stupid gun. And I'm starving."

Some things would never change, Mike thought.

Off in the distance, the majestic sound of a bull elk's bugle cut through the autumn air. Mike smiled to himself peacefully. He couldn't have been happier.

"C'mon, Dad. What's the deal? How do we get this sucker outta here?"

The older man bent over and felt the elk with his hands, testing its weight. "Well, he's pretty big, so I'll just dress him right here. We'll strap as much as we can onto our backs, but we'll probably have to make two trips."

"Awww, Dad, you mean we have to carry it out?"

ABOUT THE AUTHOR

Ethan Campbell attends Ainsworth High School in Ainsworth, Nebraska. He plays center on his school's football team and throws shotput and discus in track. Speech team, acting in plays, working as a radio DJ, and membership in Fellowship of Christian Athletes and Bulldog Buddies (similar to Big Brothers) keep him busy. He has also won an award for his writing in Nebraska's Literature Festival. Like the characters in this story, he and his father take annual elk-hunting trips to Colorado.

They were three best friends in a perfect childhood summer. Then Jason broke the news . . .

Spearhead Days

by ABIGAIL SMIGEL

With a loud "Humph," I slumped down into the pile of garden sacks in the back of the garage. The stench of old gardening tools, fertilizer, and trash seeped into my head as I shifted my position to a more comfortable one. I grabbed an old lime sack to cover myself before it was too late: he was coming and I knew it. The unmistakable sound of his feet getting closer. Suddenly a pail of rotten tulip bulbs fell onto the table near me, and then to the floor with a crash. A cloud of dust forced me to let out a small sputter as I burrowed deeper into the heap of unexplored belongings. I knew I would be found in a minute . . . if only I could reach that old sled to cover . . . "GOTCHA!"

I screamed, and in the confusion, that sled landed directly on my left baby toe. I hollered some more. "How did you find me?" I cried out.

"My magic spearhead showed me," he said. Laughing hysterically, he held the prize as it shined in the light of the garage. Jason rolled on the floor laughing as I emerged with a layer of crud covering my face, body, and clothing. Tears were streaming down my face, creating a muddy mess as he began to laugh even harder. Between gasps he hollered, "Come . . . into the . . . garage! I . . . got her!" Looming in the afternoon light of the doorway was another figure, seized with laughter.

"It's not funny!" I screamed. "My foot is broken, and all you jerks can do is sit there and laugh!" I was furious! I brushed myself off with one large swipe and stormed out of the garage—well, actually, I more like hobbled out. Making my way toward our tree on the outside of the court, I swung up to the bottom branch and clambered to the top where Brad and Jason couldn't reach me.

You see, being a girl has its advantages. I could climb to the highest part of the tree because I was so much lighter than the guys. Perched in "my spot," I looked to the garage across the street and saw the two idiots rolling on the grass. They probably thought that this was the funniest thing in the world. Well, it wasn't. I removed my shoe and set it on one of the sturdier branches at the top of the tree. My baby toe had swollen to the size of my big toe and had become a color purple to match my Miss Piggy T-shirt. "Shut up!" I shouted at them. They continued to wallow in the grass like the slimy pigs they were. Looking down at them, I wondered how I had ever wanted to be friends with them.

Brad and I had known each other since we were born, but we didn't meet up with Jason until we were at least five or six. Jason always used to hang out with Bill, another neighbor, and we would always have snowball fights or water-gun wars against each other. One time Brad fell down in the middle of one of our water-gun wars, and Jason went charging over with his gun. I quickly ran to Brad's rescue, but Jason wasn't trying to hurt him anymore, just help him up.

Once the three of us decided that we were friends, we did everything together. We would go to the field in back of Brad's house and catch bees together. After a while, we got bored with that and started catching them with our hands instead. None of us got stung but the thought of it made us sick. Sometimes we would make up things to do when there was nothing else. You know that time during the summer when everything stands still, and you can't find anything to do? Well, one day Jason got this bright idea that we should run around the neighborhood screaming things into the mailboxes, so that when the mailman came to deliver the mail he would hear our echoes. It didn't work. Then we decided to leave presents in the mailbox for our wonderful mailman (such as spiders, ants, and any other small creatures that we could find). Usually, they either all escaped or were dead by the time the mailman arrived, and didn't make the slightest impression on him.

Science intrigued us more than anything else. One time, for his birthday, Brad got a dissecting kit from his grandmother. It had a frog, a crayfish, a few bugs, and so many prongs and knives we didn't know what to do with ourselves. Fortunately, Brad offered to let us help him dissect the creatures. We got right to work. Starting with the frog, we immediately sliced down its

skin to see all the organs inside. It was so cool! We
continued looking through the entire body until I decided to cut open its mouth a little more so we could
see the esophagus. Well, I must've been applying too
much pressure, because *plink!* there went the tongue
clear across the driveway and into a bush. We had a
good laugh that day!

I was shaken back to reality as everything in my
view began to toss and swerve. I figured we must be
experiencing the worst earthquake in history. Looking
down, I quickly realized that I shouldn't be so naive:
the pigs were shaking the tree as hard as they possibly could. "What do you think, I'm gonna fly safely
down to the ground as soon as I lose my grip on this
tree?" I shouted down to them.

"No," Brad yelled. "We thought we could dissect
you as soon as you landed on the asphalt."

"Ha ha!" I screamed. They stopped shaking the
tree and let me climb down. I jumped to the ground,
landing on my still usable right foot, and took a swing
at both of them. I ended up knocking Jason down, but
Brad quickly dodged my attempt to pummel him. At
once, we all began wrestling and didn't stop for about
ten minutes, when the scrapes and bruises became un-
bearable. We sat there staring at one another, exhausted
and breathing heavily. I noticed that the spearhead on
the string around Jason's neck seemed to be breathing with him. Brad suggested we go burn some ants
with the new magnifying glass that he got from his
grandfather. I squealed "Yeah!" with delight, and both
of us were up and ready to go. But Jason just sat there
and mumbled, "I can't."

"Why not? You don't wanna hurt duh poor widdle ants?" Brad mocked in a baby tone.

"Shut up," Jason said. "It's not that," he started slowly. "I have to go pack."

"Awesome!" I exclaimed. "Where are you going? Florida, the beach, California . . . ?"

"No," he interrupted, "I'm not going on vacation. I'm moving."

Brad and I just stood there, dumbfounded. From the look on his face, I knew that he was thinking the same thing I was—What were we going to do without our best friend? "Where? How long? When?" I asked him, confused.

"I'm moving to Hawaii next week," he stated simply, as if he'd rehearsed it all last night.

Next week, I thought to myself. *That's so soon.*

"I have to go," he ended, and ran down the street.

Wait! There were so many questions I wanted to ask, and he'd only answered one of them. I was losing my best friend, and he couldn't even stay to tell me anything. Brad turned to me and said, "Let's go burn ants." He said it as if he didn't care, but I knew he did. He just didn't want to let it show—the way Jason was acting, also. I hate boys.

For the rest of the day we just sat there letting the ants escape if they wanted to and not saying much of anything except for "Yes," "No," and "Uh-huh." I couldn't stop thinking about it that whole day—the rest of the week, for that matter. What were we going to do when he was gone? After all, he was the one who showed us how to have fun.

At the dinner table one day during the week, I asked my mom why they were moving, and she told me that his dad had been offered a job there that would pay twice as much as the one he had here in Maryland. I told her that I thought his dad was a selfish pig, and she sent me to my room without the rest of my dinner.

I didn't see Jason for that whole week. I tried to go over to see him, but his mother always told me that he was busy packing or didn't have time to come play with me. I couldn't help wondering why he wouldn't come see me and Brad. One day Brad and I were sitting out in the court, throwing rocks down the hill, when we saw a familiar figure coming up the street. We just stayed sitting, pretending that we didn't see him. He walked right up to us and sat down and began to throw rocks also. For the longest time, all of us just sat there in a daze while our eyes followed the rocks tumbling down the hill. Finally, Jason broke the silence. "I'm sorry, you guys," he began. "There was nothing I could have done to stop this move."

"You could have told us sooner!" Brad blurted. I looked away from them both, not knowing what to say. I looked past the field to the trees and then gazed at the horizon where the sun was setting. All the colors of the sky were melding together to show the absolute beauty of the entire day. That is when I realized that I was going to miss him more than I ever thought possible.

I turned to Jason. "Will you write every day?"

"Of course," he said. "I will tell you guys all about everything and will come back to visit all the time." Suddenly I felt relieved and wasn't so mad anymore. It wasn't like I was never going to see him ever again.

"I have to go now. The plane leaves in an hour and a half and we have to drive there." All three of us became locked in a seemingly endless moment of silence. Then he was gone, leaving behind him all the memories that we shared together. As Brad and I walked back to our houses, I glanced one more time at the hill we had just left and saw something shiny on the ground. It was Jason's spearhead. I put it in my pocket and looked up at the horizon. I realized that the sun was not only setting on that day, but on a special part of my life.

ABOUT THE AUTHOR

Abigail Smigel wrote this story as a student at Watkins Mill High School in her hometown of Gaithersburg, Maryland. She plans to major in marine biology. Her special interests include skiing, swimming, and participating in gymnastics competitions.

Kenston High School
17425 Snyder Road
Chagrin Falls, OH 44023-2728

Would it kill him to write a happy ending?

The Misunderstood Adolescent Writer

by JOHN TRAVER

The adolescent writer sat at his keyboard, his mind burgeoning with images as the words paraded before him on the computer screen. "Ha ha!" he laughed aloud as he thought of the perfect ironic twist to end his story. Perhaps he could not control the number of pimples on his face, but he could control fully the fates of his characters, who no doubt wished their creator had chosen less morbid destinies for them. Of course, fewer than half the main characters could ever even have the opportunity to dispute their fates, since most had been laid to rest by the end of their respective stories.

This plethora of deaths was not because the adolescent writer, Don Raven by name, had an overabundance of blood lust. It was merely that his mind just happened to have a knack for thinking of deeply saddening, ironic deaths for characters, animal or human, male or female. Perhaps part of the reason was that he hadn't had a girlfriend since kindergarten; almost anyone would have a general cynicism toward life when he realized that he'd reached his girlfriend-getting peak when he was six—and had deteriorated from there.

Perhaps it could be considered ironic that the more bizarre and saddening a character's death was, the happier Don was. He did not look upon it as rejoicing over others' manufactured misfortunes; he looked upon it, rather, as "artistic appreciation." And, upon typing his latest object of artistic appreciation, he printed out the story, naturally forgetting, in his excitement and haste, to use the spell checker.

"Mom, I wrote a new story," he called from his room. "Wanna read it?" His mother was an English teacher, as well as his guinea pig for trying out each of his new masterpieces. He ran downstairs to where she was correcting her students' papers. "Mom, would you like to read my story?" The question was delivered in a way that left no room for his mother's interpretation as to what her reaction should be: one of boundless jubilation, jubilation that could never be matched until she was blessed with the opportunity of reading yet *another* of his stories.

"Not right now, Don," she said. "I have too much schoolwork to do."

"Funny, those look like stories you're correcting."

"Yes, they are."

"Funny, I have a story right here that could also be corrected. Unless, of course, it is inferior to those you are already reading. Or unless the writer is not important enough to spend time reading when there are others who are so much more interesting and lovable."

He gave her a look almost as sorrowful as his characters would have given *him* right before he brought about their demise.

"Sorry, but I can't."

Don disagreed profusely with this assessment but found his mother's pile of papers too big a mountain for even *his* faith to move. So he went off to his room . . . and immediately began to plot his real-life story. *Hmmmm*, he pondered. He badly wanted her opinion on this story because he hoped it was good enough to enter in a contest, just like his last story, for which he should be getting the acceptance (or—shudder—rejection) letter any day now. In fact, he thought automatically of its being a rejection slip, because he had read, concerning successful authors, that despondency added to "the creative process," and he certainly did not want to interfere with the creative process. In fact, he was so enamored of the idea that poverty and sadness inspire writing (he relied on Poe for his proof) that he felt he had to tone down the happiness that was in his life by thinking of all those who were happier than he.

Who are the couples in school? There's Brenda and Fred. I was actually beginning to think that maybe Brenda liked me, even down to the very hour before she asked Fred out. I get better grades than Fred, but I guess that doesn't matter to Brenda or the other girls in my class. No, it's a fact—even my own characters don't like me. Who else has a girlfriend? Bob, Alan, and . . . He would finally stop this self-torture after he had thought of enough happy twosomes to fuel his capacity for causing torment in his characters.

But now Don's creative energy was directed toward

getting his mother to read his story. Luckily, the solution became readily apparent: *All I have to do is change the phrase 'By Don Raven.' I can insert the name of one of Mom's students under the title, and then she'll read the story! I'll admit that it was really by me at the end!* Then he realized that if his mother spent all that time reading his story under false pretenses, she might get angry, and his fate could end up being just as morbid as his characters'. That was one twist of irony he wished to avoid. Finally he decided to let the first half of the page go by without any identification. That would be enough to get her really into the story, before seeing: "Actually, this isn't by (insert student's name). This is by your son, Don. He very much wants you to read this story. Is this the only way he can get you to read his stories? Is this the only way *your own son* can get you as an audience for one of his creations—to pretend to be one of your students? Are these the depths to which you have forced him to sink? Wouldn't you rather read one of his stories than what you've been reading? And aren't you too enmeshed in his story, which continues on the next page, to stop now?"

Don knew he was taking a chance with this deception, but, after preparing the manuscript, he waited for his parents to go to bed and, chuckling evilly to himself, placed it below the one his mother had already started. "She'll correct it in the morning," he chortled. "By the time she realizes it's not by one of her students, it will be too late!" Don then retired to bed, his work accomplished, his plot complete.

Sadly, he wasn't expecting to be awakened at 5:30 A.M. by his mother, who was in the practice of rising at 4:00 A.M. to correct papers. "I read your story," she said.

"Um . . . good . . . good . . . night," Don replied, pushing his head into the comforting pillow. While being rudely awakened did spark the creative process, Don preferred methods less painful.

"You tricked me," she said. "I thought it was by one of my students."

"Well, that's kind of what I was expecting," Don mumbled, attempting to return to his slumber, which was quite difficult to do since she kept on talking.

"This whole thing is really funny, Don. Think about it—an English teacher's son pretending to be one of her students just to get his mother to do for him what she does without question for her students. That would make a good story."

"Fine," Don said. "But what about the real story? The one I wrote?" That was the part Don was more interested in.

"I just don't understand, Don, why you have to be so dark and depressing. Why don't you write happy things?"

"Because I don't get ideas for happy stories," Don answered. "Besides, happy stories are just too—too happy. You just keep expecting something bad to happen, and nothing ever does, so they're anticlimactic."

"We'll talk about that later," she said. Never mind the fact that she had awakened Don from a very dandy sleep, no doubt what she had decided would be the price for his deception.

So Don attempted to return to his slumber and was finally able to achieve some uneasy sleep for approximately thirty minutes until his alarm clock woke him.

He passed nonchalantly through the daily school grind
until he returned home, to receive a letter telling him
the good news: his latest contest entry had been rejected, but he shouldn't feel too discouraged because
"sometimes a story or novel is turned down as many
as twenty times before it is finally published." One of
the comments that the rejection letter bore was that
his story was "too morbid at the end."

Don was anxious for his mother to come home, to
ease the pain of rejection and to get her reaction to
his latest creative endeavor. Without sympathy, she responded, "I'd have to say the same thing that your rejection letter said: everything you write is too morbid."

"Wow, what a great way for me to find this out!
And now I'm supposed to be able to think of something uplifting, right after getting my story rejected!
Piece of cake! But wait. I've got it! I'll write about
what just happened! About the misunderstood adolescent writer whom everybody oppresses and pres-
sures into thinking happy thoughts, thus making him
even gloomier! It will be easy to write a happy story
with that plot!"

The mother interrupted her son. "Don, no one likes
gloom—period! Write a funny story about your rejection!"

"Oh, of course," Don said, still trying to recover
from the astonishing blow that his ironic stories weren't
appreciated by man or mother. "How about I also send
in a funny story about death! There's a long tradition
of funny material there, you know."

"Don, I really think that's why you're getting rejected. Your writing's very good; it's just that if you

wrote about happier things or had slightly happier endings—"

"Fine!" Don huffed. Internally, he could hear his characters (who still lived) cheering his mother on.

Yet he refused to surrender entirely. "I'll write one happy story and send it in—to the *Merlyn's Pen* Short Story Contest, no less! And if they reject it, I'll go back to writing the good stuff about doom, gloom, and the tomb!" Don stared defiantly at his mother.

"And if they accept it, then you will write—"

"Um . . . mostly gloomy stories, but I'll also do a few happy ones, just to keep my readers happy . . ."

Allow me to interrupt here. My name is George. I'm one of Don's up-and-coming characters, and I feel it only fair to warn you that if this story doesn't get published, I shall be his next victim. I don't want to make you feel pressured, but if Don's story isn't chosen . . . Well, let's not go into that! Suffice it to say that, for once, my fate isn't in Don's hands, but in yours. And by the way, I'm a koala, if that makes you care a little more for my endangered welfare. A very cute koala, I might add.

ABOUT THE AUTHOR

John Traver lives in Philadelphia and is a student at Philadelphia-Montgomery Christian Academy in Erdenheim, Pennsylvania. He is especially interested in reading, writing, and learning unusual vocabulary words. Other pastimes include playing the piano and participating in his church youth group.

Vivid memories of a child's terror—
and a father's love.

Hawks

by CAROLYN JENNINGS

We walked down the concourse toward my dad's gate. He held my hand and was constantly adjusting his pace so I could keep up. Mom walked along with us, holding Dad's other hand. We arrived at the gate and sat down to wait for people to begin boarding. I remember running up to the windows and staring at the huge airplanes and the little trucks that sped around carrying luggage and food to the planes. It looked kind of like my ant farm, where the worker ants brought everything to the queen, only the trucks seemed so tiny next to those big, lumbering planes. I could see a plane getting ready to take off, but its wings weren't flapping like the birds I always watched as they flew over the river.

A booming sound interrupted my observations. I jumped as I felt the ground move in time with the roaring. I ran to Daddy and grabbed his arm.

"What is it? What is it?" I cried. It reminded me of the lions on television, only worse. Why was the ground shaking?

"Oh, Daddy, let's go! I'm scared," I said through a scrunched-up face, the tears raining down.

He picked me up and hugged me tightly, practically yelling over the roar, saying he loved me and would miss me so much. I didn't understand what he was saying. I just wanted to get out of there.

"I wanna go home!" He put me down and gave Mom a long hug. I couldn't figure out what was going on. Dad was hugging everybody and that roaring kept shaking the ground! I was terrified.

Mom was crying as Dad patted me on the head and walked toward the door. "No, Daddy, don't go over there! It's going to get you!" Mom held me tight in her arms as I tried to save Daddy from IT—whatever IT was. He finally went through the door and was gone.

We stood at the window and watched as the roaring slowly faded and the plane was off the ground and soaring in the air—without even flapping its wings! It had stolen Daddy . . . Mom said he would be back. She took my hand and we walked, quietly, through the airport and out to the car.

The next few weeks were quiet, oh so quiet. We telephoned Dad every night, and he and Mom would talk about the new job and everything that was going on. Mom was always upset after these conversations; she said things weren't working out as they had planned.

It was really boring. I didn't like just *talking* to Dad. We had more fun when we were together outside, fishing or playing ball. I missed him.

Every night after dinner I would go down to the dock, the way Dad and I always used to, and watch the turtles in the water. I poked them with sticks even though Dad always told me not to. I just wanted to say hello. The water was covered with fish spit. At least, that's what Dad always called the foam that comes when the water gets rough. I sat for a while watching the sun go down and the lightning bugs come out, but then I had to head for home or Mom would get mad. As I was jumping on the molehills on my way home, I could hear a plane getting nearer and nearer. The rumble turned into a roar and I began to run. *Faster, faster*—or it would get me! I had to escape from this beast before it took me away, too. I landed on my back step just as the roaring was starting to fade. Close call!

Every other week the planes would swoop down low and I would fly home, faster than the plane could go, narrowly escaping each time. Mom tried to explain that we lived along a flight path of the air force base and that every other week they flew over while practicing their maneuvers, but I could never understand. It was obvious that they were after me, trying to catch me and take me away.

Night after night I would go down to the dock and sit on the edge, being really quiet, and wait. After a while the fish would swim under my feet and I could watch them in their silent, peaceful world. Lucky fish—they didn't have to worry about big monsters roaring into their lives, chasing them and taking away *their* daddies! Then the plane would come and I would hightail it home, knowing that once I got there everything would be safe and secure.

One night I was watching the minnows and poking a turtle that was trying to climb up the piling. I was totally involved in trying to get that turtle back down into the water and away from the dock because there were several hawks flying above. I tried to scare them off so the little turtle could have time to get home, but they didn't seem to even notice me. I returned to the dock and with my stick was pushing the turtle along, away from the mean predators hanging above, when suddenly I felt a gentle touch on my head. A familiar voice said, "You know you shouldn't be poking the turtles."

"I remember. I really do, but the turtle should go back home because a hawk could take him away and then eat him all up for dinner," I explained.

The familiar voice laughed, and arms encircled me in a great big hug. Just then, the far-off rumble began and I started to tremble. When I told him about the plane and what it could do to us, he held me even tighter. I cowered, shaking in his arms as the plane flew over. Then it was gone, and again it was quiet. It was that simple. The pain only lasted a moment.

Daddy said that the job hadn't worked out, that we were going to stay here. He was home for good.

So we just sat there, in the purpling dusk, and watched as the turtle inched back home. When both turtle and sun had disappeared, we too got up, and, with my hand enfolded in his, wended our way home. I noticed the hawks, quietly patrolling the night. Sailing above in sweeping beauty, they no longer looked mean at all. The turtle was safe.

ABOUT THE AUTHOR

Carolyn Jennings lives in Pendleton, Kentucky, and attends Oldham County High School in Buckner. She has played on soccer teams since the fifth grade and now coaches a team for little boys. She also enjoys volunteering at a hospital, participating in church groups, and swimming. Last summer Carrie was selected as a Governor's Scholar for the State of Kentucky and helped out at Habitat for Humanity.

Slices of life, both local and global.

Second Glances

by GERARD GOLDEN

A NERD'S EPIPHANY

He was wearing sandals that were too big. And there was a flap of plastic hanging from the bottom of his right heel that clicked annoyingly as he walked in. The sandals showcased a crusty case of athlete's foot that was slowly but steadily creeping up to his ankles.

Fungi weren't limited to his feet, either. In fact, as he sat there in math class after playing softball in gym, his armpits reeked of a heinous odor which quickly spread throughout the room. To make the situation even worse, he would insist on reaching his arm across the pathway between our desks to pick up his runaway pencil, or stretching to the stars as he yawned violently during the lesson on trigonometry functions.

His tight, curly hair was so saturated with sweat that the greasy mixture of too many pore excrements dripped slow, isolated drops onto his torn gray T-shirt. The sweat stains were perfect matches for the pizza stains on the left leg of his camouflage army shorts.

Long, solitary hairs on his face simply highlighted his almost artistic carelessness. The truth is, he didn't grow his sparse, disgusting beard because he thought it looked good. It was probably because he was just too lazy to shave, or, given his spasticity, feared he would cut himself with the razor.

A repulsive creature, do you say? Well, every day when I lean back to glance at my future bride (although we've not yet met), she is gazing helplessly and hopelessly with love at this freak. She stares with a dumb look of fantasy, and an oncoming rocket couldn't steal her attention long enough to wipe off that wide, closed-lipped smile.

So I now have a plan. From this point on, I will not bathe, shave, or wear clean clothes. I'll be a stud yet.

STUPID

Sometimes I wish I were stupid. And I don't mean your everyday kid who fails tests here and there or even classes here and there. I mean really stupid, beyond repair. A real idiot. Then I wouldn't have to worry about the earth suddenly losing its force of gravity and drifting out into space where I would suffocate and die. I wouldn't even know what gravity is.

I wouldn't think twice before getting into the passenger seat of a car late at night and wondering if I have a faulty seat belt or if there's a drunk driver around the corner, or if the fumes from the car in front of me are coming in through my window and giving me cancer. I'd be a drunk driver myself and be too bombed to care about my safety.

I wouldn't feel guilty throwing out the leftovers of my huge helping of turkey on Thanksgiving, thinking about the people starving in Somalia and others within miles who are dreaming of getting just a taste. I would not have even heard of Planet Somalia and I wouldn't understand why they couldn't just go to the drive-thru at the local McDonald's.

I wouldn't worry about school tests and term papers and have terrible insomnia every night—because I would fail them all, and then fall into beautifully deep dreamland.

ABOUT THE AUTHOR

Gerard Golden is a student at Clarkstown High School North, in New City, New York.

All this fun, and money too!

Perfect Angels

by Kari Haworth

It was Friday night and I was walking up the driveway, getting ready for the baby-sitting job that loomed in front of me. Actually, I didn't know anything about the Rockers except that they had two boys and a girl. The girl was five, and the boys were six and three. I also knew that their parents were desperate for babysitters because of the way they begged me on the phone to come.

I walked up to the door and rang their doorbell, observing all of their welcome signs. Above the door, a sign said, "The Rockers Welcome You." The doormat said, "Welcome To Our Home." The mailbox, in gold letters, said simply, "Welcome All." I smiled. They certainly loved people. I started to knock when a blond boy wearing a pair of old jeans, a shirt that had "Watch Out—HERE I COME" on the front, and a mean scowl opened the door and demanded to know who I was. I could tell already—he was going to be trouble.

"I'm the babysitter. My name is Kari. What's yours?"

He ignored my greeting and just stood there staring. What a welcoming committee! Finally, he decided to talk.

"Mom, the babysitter's here."

A flustered woman who was trying to fix her disheveled hair and straighten her nylons while picking up toys in her path came to the door with her other two children behind her.

"OH. You must be KARI. So glad to SEE you. Thank you SO much for coming. PLEASE come in."

I walked in and the children all backed up about five feet. Great. I could tell that they were going to just love me.

"Children, this is KARI. Can we say HI?"

"Hi," said a girl with yellow hair, a pink dress, and shiny white shoes.

Mrs. Rocker practically fell over with delight at her daughter's greeting.

"That's ANGELA. She won't give you ANY problems. Will you, sweetheart?"

Angela turned to me and glared so Mrs. Rocker couldn't see, then turned to her mother and smiled charmingly.

"Of course not, Mommy."

Mrs. Rocker melted. "What an ANGEL you are, princess!"

She pointed to the boy who had greeted me at the door and who was now leaning against a closet. He was a direct contrast to the perfect Angela.

"That's Billy," she said, a little less enthused. "Say HI, dear."

A smirk broke out on his face. "Hi, dear."

He started laughing hysterically and Mrs. Rocker joined him.

"Billy has SUCH a sense of humor!"

Yeah, wonderful. I guess different parents call it different things.

"And THIS is Petey. Where's Petey? Billy, WHAT did you do with him?"

As Billy turned away, Angela volunteered her information.

"I tried to stop him, Mommy, but Billy put Petey in the closet."

"Billy!" Mrs. Rocker ran over to the closet and brought out a three-year-old boy with curly brown hair and red overalls.

"Are you OK, Petey?"

Petey folded his arms and sat down on the floor.

"NO!"

For a small kid, Petey had a large lung capacity. Mrs. Rocker turned to Billy, who was trying to sneak away.

"Billy, you're going to have to say you're SORRY to Petey."

We all waited.

"Billy?"

"I'm not Billy. I'm Indiana Jones," he said in a high-pitched tough voice.

"Well that's FINE, honey, but you're going to have to learn to say you're SORRY."

She sighed and looked at me.

"You'll HAVE to excuse Billy. He had a glass of KOOL-AID last week and he ALWAYS gets this way when he's had too much SUGAR."

I smiled. Great. In a couple of years he'll be shav-

ing the neighbors' cats. I looked again at Billy, who
was pretending to kill Petey with a toy gun. I was wondering whether or not I should turn and run. Then,
all of a sudden, Mrs. Rocker decided to give me thou-
sands of instructions in "fast-forward" mode.

"Bed for Angela and Petey at 8:00, Billy 8:30 unless he acts up one bedtime story no TV read books—
they love stories—wash face and brush teeth before
bedtime no fighting Petey needs help putting on his
pajamas Angela always sleeps with her pink doll Petey
needs his bedtime light on take away Billy's safari hat
before he goes to bed or he'll sleep on it only one
s-n-a-c-k if they remember I think that's about it."

Well, I'm so glad. Mothers seem to think babysitters have computers for brains. I'd be lucky if I remembered their names and bedtimes. I tried not to
look too confused as I listened to her. After she was
finished, she looked up at the ceiling (probably pray-
ing for me), then looked quickly at her watch.

"Oh MY, look at the TIME. I must go. Goodbye,
darlings. BEHAVE yourselves and listen to Kari. Bye
bye."

After she left, I turned to the kids, who were all
watching the door. Angela sat smiling with her hands
folded in her lap, Billy leaned against the opposite wall
with an annoyed look on his face, and Petey stood
right in front of the door and stared at the doorknob.
I was about to ask them what they were doing when
in came Mrs. Rocker, giving kisses she forgot to give
before and exclaiming how sorry she was to leave them,
how sad it made her feel, how she'd come back very
soon with a present for each one of them, and how
much she loved them. Before she tore herself away,

she succeeded in getting Petey to start begging her not to leave, Angela to say how much she loved her mommy one million times, and Billy to put an even bigger scowl on his face than before. Great. This outpouring of love was going to make my job about ten times harder.

After she finally left, I turned to the kids and gave my best hi-I'm-the-babysitter smile. They all stared at me blankly.

"What would you like to do?" I asked cheerfully. First mistake. I shouldn't have given them a choice. It's much smarter to say: "This is what we're doing."

"Watch TV," answered Billy.

"Sorry, your mommy said, 'No TV tonight.'"

"I want to watch TV," whined Petey.

"Sorry, guys. Why don't we do something else?"

"NO!" roared Billy. "I'm going to watch TV."

"You wanna bet?" He glared at me and I glared back. I was losing my patience with this over-sugared kid.

"You aren't my mommy or my daddy."

Thank the Lord for small favors.

"No, I'm not, but I'm in charge."

"Who cares?"

I chose to ignore that remark because I didn't want to lose my temper so soon. I decided to change the subject.

"I know," I said enthusiastically. "Let's read a book, OK?"

"That's boring," whined Petey.

It seemed as if all he ever did was whine.

"Do we have to?" asked Angela.

"If we have to read another stupid book, I'm leaving," declared Billy.

That was tempting.

"Look, guys, your mom said you liked books." Actually, I shouldn't have listened because I know better. Mothers just want their children to seem intellectual by saying how much they love books.

"When's Mommy coming home?" asked Petey.

"Late. After you're in bed."

"I want her NOW," he said, his voice quivering. I watched in horror as his face contorted into a pout. Oh no. He was going to throw a temper tantrum—something I definitely could not handle. Nothing can be done to stop a tantrum once it's started, and waiting for it to end is a nightmare. I had to stop this from happening.

"You'll see her in the morning," I said quickly.

"Yeah, Petey, so be quiet," Angela added.

Petey stuck his tongue out at her.

"YOU be quiet, An-ge-la!" he said with authority.

I reached down to pick up a book when Angela grabbed it and threw it, hitting Petey on the shoulder. I stood there, stunned, not knowing how to react. I turned to Angela and gave her a harsh, mother-like stare as she returned to her angelic self.

"Angela! Oh, Petey, are you all right? Come here, sweetheart."

Petey came over, threw himself at my feet, and started to wail. I turned to Angela.

"Angela, what in the world did you do that for?"

"I didn't," she replied, smiling sweetly.

"Angela, don't lie to me. I saw you."

"Well," she said innocently, "Petey was mean to me. He deserved it."

She was worse than Billy! True, Billy was a monster, but at least he didn't try to cover up the fact.

"He did not deserve it. Now, you get away from him. Go and sit over there on that chair."

Her smile turned sour. "Why?" she demanded.

"Because I don't want you near Petey."

She stood still, pretending not to hear me.

"Go on, Angela."

She sat down where she was and smoothed her dress. It's maddening to have kids ignore you! How do her parents stand her? Simple—they're too dense to see past her angelic face.

"Angela, go over there and sit down."

"I will not!" she said stubbornly.

"Angela," I said in a warning tone to which she paid no attention.

I went over to where she was sitting, picked her up, and put her where I wanted her to be. She started giggling.

"This isn't funny, Angela," I said in a low voice, my face turning red from anger. "If this were funny, I would be laughing."

She looked at me and started to cry.

"I don't like you."

I hate it when kids start to cry on me. I softened, feeling guilty for being such a horrible person.

"Come on, Angela. You've got to learn not to hurt people like that."

I pleaded with her to stop crying. Granted, it wasn't very good discipline, but what could I do? All I could think about was her parents coming home and her saying: "She was so mean, Mommy! She made me cry." Finally, Angela wiped her eyes. That was good enough. All of a sudden, it became quiet. Too quiet. I looked around. Petey was playing with his shoelaces and Angela was pouting, but where was . . .

"Billy?"

No answer. I was worried. Not that I was concerned for his safety. I was concerned about my own.

"Billy?"

I looked in the closet. He wasn't there. I left the room, looked down the hall, and saw him—standing on their off-white couch with his dirty shoes. I almost had a heart attack.

"Billy," I said, trying to control myself, "get off there."

"I'm not Billy, I'm Jaws," he said, jumping up and down. I cringed. With every jump he was probably making a black mark.

"Ha, ha, ha." He laughed in a sinister way and started to bite one of the pillows. Cute kid. Really cute. If he were my kid, I'd give him tranquilizers. I went over and took him by the arm.

"C'mon, get off the couch."

"I'm a shark. I'm Jaws."

He started to hum the *Jaws* theme and I lifted him off the couch. While I was lifting him down, he bit me on the arm. Fortunately for him, it didn't break my skin, or I would have made him eat one of those pillows. I was mad enough as it was.

"Billy! Why did you do that? Who do you think you are?"

Dumb question. I knew what he was going to say.

"I'm a shark. I'm Jaws."

I held myself back. I'm not a killer by nature, but I was afraid I might become one. I kept telling myself I just wasn't used to overactive children. I smiled at him in a calm way.

"You're dead if you try that again."

"I'll beat your brains out," he said triumphantly. I started to explain to him the Law of Sizes.

"I'm bigger than you, so I wouldn't try anything if I were you. Got it, Jaws?"

He started to hum the *Jaws* theme again and ran off. I sighed and thought about his parents, who had to go through this every day and night. Oh well, it was their fault. Something obviously went wrong with their parenting. I glanced at the clock. It said 7:50—the most glorious numbers in the world. I went into the play room. Angela and Petey were in the exact same positions as they were when I left them.

"OK, kids, it's time for bed. Angela, Petey, come on."

"Why?" asked Petey.

"Because it's time for bed."

"But why?"

Oh, no, here come the questions. He was exactly the right age for the "questioning stage." I hate stages. They're all annoying.

"Because it's eight o'clock."

"Why?"

"Because the clock says so."

"Why?"

"Because Father Time tells it to say so."

"Who's Father Time?"

"He works with Mother Nature. You see, together they look at the universe, the axis of the earth, the degree of the moon, and the angle of the sun, and write all of that data down on an ipsiluta chart which calculates the umber dictum. Mother Nature interprets this and shocnacs it to Father Time, who whispers it to clocks around the world. Do you understand?"

"Yes," said Petey.

I had him trapped. I know—I'm a terrible person to lie to an innocent child. Really, I was only looking out for him. If he had asked any more questions, he might have gotten hoarse. Anyway, I prefer to call it a "bedtime story."

"You know what, Petey? You're one of the few people who knows this very important information. Let me tell you another secret. Sometimes, Father Time comes to these very important people like you, and talks to them in their sleep! I have a good idea. Why don't you go brush your teeth and wash your face and get into your pajamas. Then, come back really quickly and go to bed so Father Time will visit you. OK?"

"OK. And I can dress myself."

"But your mom said . . ." I stopped. "OK, Petey, you can dress yourself."

I really didn't care. Just as long as he went to bed. I looked at Angela and Billy, who were giggling.

"None of that's true, babysitter. I know. I'm smart."

"Good for you." I ended the conversation. It was much harder to trick kids their age.

"Angela, bedtime."

"I'm not tired." I knew that. Kids are never tired.

"Angela, you've got to get ready for bed."

"I'm not tired."

"Angela, don't you want to get into your pretty nightgown?" I said, trying to get to her through her vanity.

"No."

"Wouldn't you like to get some sleep so you can

get up bright and early tomorrow morning?"

"No." I should have known. Kids get up early, regardless of how much sleep they manage to get.

"Wouldn't you like for me to tell your mom you were perfect for me?"

"Yes." Aha! She couldn't risk her spotless reputation.

"Then I suggest you go get ready for bed or I'll give her a bad report."

"Oh, OK."

"Thank you, Angela. I'm so glad you're being so helpful," I called after her sarcastically.

In about twenty seconds, Angela and Petey both were back. Angela had toothpaste all over her face, and Petey's pajamas were on backwards and inside out.

"You two look great! I'm so glad you're old enough to get ready for bed so nicely. Now, if you'll run and jump into your beds, I won't read you another boring bedtime story, OK?"

"Yeah!" They ran off. That was too easy. I faced my last challenge: Indiana Jones/Jaws/Billy.

"How about you?"

"I'm busy," he said, picking up a G.I. Joe.

"That's too bad, because it's your bedtime."

"I'm not tired." I could imagine.

"Well, I know, but you're going to have to go to sleep. Don't you want to be big and strong?"

"I already am."

I could tell this was going to be loads of fun. I immediately resorted to begging. Why not?

"Billy, pleeeeeease go to bed?"

"No."

"Billy, your mommy would be very upset if she

knew you were staying up this late."

"No, she wouldn't." He was probably right. She'd just blame the sugar and let him stay up. I, on the other hand, couldn't stand the kid and wanted him asleep.

"Don't you want to be as strong as Popeye?"

"Popeye's a wimp."

What kind of kid thinks Popeye's a wimp? I used to idolize him. What's wrong with kids today, anyway?

"Hey—I know. Let's do an Ulikbogwa ritual." Here comes another "bedtime story."

"What's that?"

Well, at least I got him to respond. But then I had to think fast of what exciting ritual the "Ulikbogwa" people do. I could hardly think of what a ritual was.

"It's where the babysitter picks up the kid and runs as fast as she can to his room and throws him on the bed and if he goes to sleep right away, he's made the king. Are you ready?"

"No. I don't want to . . ."

"GO!" I shouted as I grabbed him up, ran into the room and threw him on the bed. I started to chant "sleep" over and over again and danced around the room. Billy was staring at me with wide eyes. Good! I was confusing him.

"Now go to sleep really quick, Billy."

"But I don't—"

"You can't mess up the ritual after it has started. It's very bad luck."

I started to chant again and danced out the door, closing it and turning off the light behind me. A very convincing performance, I must say. But wait until Billy tells them the story. They'll think I went crazy! Maybe

I did. Who wouldn't? Billy's annoying little voice interrupted my thoughts.

"Babysitter?"

I didn't answer. I was thinking of what to say.

"Babysitter!"

"Billy! You can't talk either or you'll mess up everything and you wouldn't want to do that, would you?"

He was quiet for about ten seconds. A record for him. Then he started banging on the wall. I ignored it. I was too worn out to fight with him. I went into his room a half-hour later and he was fast asleep. The Kool-Aid must have finally worn off. I took his safari hat off and put him into his pajamas. He was really dead asleep. Amazing! I went into the living room and collapsed. After about an hour, the Rockers came home. I promised myself that I wouldn't try to kill them for having such rotten children and managed to greet them with a smile.

"How were the CHILDREN?"

That's the unwritten Code of Parents. If they don't ask how their kids were, they're imposters. And, of course, I answered with the unwritten Code of Babysitters in mind: Keep your customers happy (not that I was ever coming back)!

"Oh, they were so good for me. Just perfect angels."

ABOUT THE AUTHOR

Kari Haworth lives in Sunnyvale, California, and is a student at St. Francis High School in Mountain View. Her interests are space and spacecraft. Preparing for a career in aerospace engineering, she attended a ten-day workshop at the NASA U.S. Space Academy, in Huntsville, Alabama.

Were his dreams too big to come true?

Prophets

by BRENNAN STASIEWICZ

Y ou can always follow a line, but only those who open their eyes can tie it in a knot."

Those decaying words, wafting from my grandfather's mouth like dust through sunlight, meant nothing to me. I had lost all interest in listening to the old oracle speak the ways of life. My mind was filled with the more important thoughts of a child: the everlasting questions, such as the size of Frankie Perbleman's giant horny toad, and the length of Grandpa's nose hairs. These were the only things encircling my brain, like one of those comic strip word balloons.

The thing that stuck most in my head, however, was about my friend Jim Charlton. Jim and I had been friends ever since we were pea high. Jim was a tall fellow, but not too overpowering. He kept a low profile, but his outside appearance left a long shadow. We often spent long summer nights, lying beneath the stars above the old schoolhouse, talking all deep and serious like we were two prophets from the Bible. It was there, during these nightlong chats, that I really began to see inside Jim. Through these timeless moments of truth it became apparent to me that Jim's seemingly weak outside appearance was only skin deep. If you could look inside Jim as I had, if you could have heard those bronzed words coming from his tight-lipped mouth, you'd be able to see the real Jim. The Jim who could steam his heart past any obstacle. The Jim who emptied his soul to me in sworn secrecy, above the schoolhouse shingles, beneath the innocent stars.

It was two days earlier that Jim had told me of his venture. I played along with him in this game, but, to my discredit, I didn't really believe him. I mean, who in their right mind would ever believe that anyone could do what he was planning?

"Oh, go stick it in the mud," I said as I turned away in disbelief.

"No, Pud." Pud was the natural-sounding nickname that Jim had generously given me. "I swear it on the Bible—ain't nothin' gonna stop me from it."

Still refusing to turn and face him, I spoke from the side of my mouth, "Yeah, like I ain't never heard that from you before!" But then I realized that I never had heard Jim swear to something without doing it. Discreetly, I glanced back at him.

"Aww! Pud! You know I ain't never lied about something like this, and, to the contrary, I'm quite insulted!"

I could always tell when Jim was really upset because he'd try to talk like Mrs. Buecher, our English teacher, by using big, highfalutin words and phrases.

"I'm sorry, Jim," I said, now that I saw the flaw in my thinking. "I didn't mean to insult you."

"Yeah, well, now you got me all flabbergasted!"

I looked back down to the ground, found the spot that I had been watching earlier, and forcefully cried, "Shucks! I just think you oughta think about it some more, that's all."

"Well, don't you worry 'bout it, Pud. Now you know that I ain't kiddin'. Just don't tell no one!"

"Why?" I whined with a rolling frown.

"Just don't. I'll be the one who'll tell the town, and I'll do it on . . ." Jim stopped for a moment of thought, "Independence Day. Ju–lie the Fourth!"

The days passed by like a slug through warm beer. I had promised Jim that I would not mention his surprise to anyone, but the suspense and anticipation ate through me. It was Wednesday, two days before the Fourth of July. Mama let me sleep late because we were up till 1:00, playing a wild game of Scrabble. By the time I had dressed, cleaned, and eaten, it was a little past ten. As I looked out the window, I could just feel the thick heat float by the willow tree, to the front porch, and finally take rest over the overgrown bluegrass. I sat down on the old leather recliner in the den and enjoyed the climate. We were one of the first families in town to get an air conditioner. It was able to cool almost every room, but the one that it worked best on was the den. As I sat daydreaming about the beach and cool mountaintops, I sure wasn't looking forward to the chores that were in store for me that day.

I dozed off for a second, but my flights through the Alps soon stopped when Mama entered my cooling cocoon. Before I could say a word, before Mama could say a word, I had the daily list in my face, extracting me from my state of repose. I rose from my cool throne and headed for the reality of an early July day. I stepped out the door and off the front porch, right through that stream of thick, pea soup heat, and took immediate shelter under the willow tree. Hot July mornings are probably the worst times of the year. Not only do you have the sun leeching energy from your helpless body, but you practically have to paddle through the moist air. I stepped around the gardening my mom had set forth for me to do, and decided to visit Jimmy at the malt shop in the middle of town.

I lived in a small Midwestern town called Fleamont. It was probably one of the quietest and dullest towns there had ever been in Oklahoma. Everyone knew everyone, mostly because the population never had exceeded two hundred. Nothing new ever happened except when someone died. There was nothing special about the town, nothing extraordinary, except maybe Mt. Flea. Mt. Flea was not a mountain, but rather a mound. The town took pride in this four-hundred-foot mound because out on the Midwestern plain there aren't that many geographical formations.

I opened the door to Bubba's Malt and Fine Ice Cream Shop and stepped in. Bubba, after visiting our place last summer, decided to invest in an air conditioner, too. As the dry, arctic air hit me, the change in temperature made my skin feel like it was going to crack. I staggered to the counter and practically passed out onto one of the red vinyl stools. Jim came up and asked like a polite malt boy if he could get me anything. But as soon as Bubba went in the back of the shop, he made me a free malt.

At first I was surprised by his gesture. "What in Sam Hill are you doing?" "Sam Hill" was a little something that I picked up from Pa. "If Bubba finds out, he'll fire you in a second!" Bubba might not have graduated from high school, but he was one of the smoothest guys in town. Jack McGraw and Bubba Merris, they were the closest things we had to slick, smooth-talking greasers from the city.

Jim had a cool look on his face. "So let the old fart fire me. I'm quittin' after today anyhow. Seeing as how I'm gonna be a star and everything."

"A star? Why are you thinking 'bout being a star?"

"Well, Pud, the way I see it is that there ain't no second best. You either win, or you lose. And I ain't a loser—losers ain't stars."

This was only the second time I'd heard Jim talk like this, the first being five days earlier when he told me his plan. It wasn't like him to be so grown-up about something. He always approached things in a serious manner, but this time it seemed like he wasn't just a kid with a plan, but rather an adult. I wasn't sure how to react to this new Jim, and it seemed that I never would know how to.

One thing was for sure, though. Jim's inflating head was just ballooning out all over the place. Overwhelmed by this transformation in my friend, I just sat back and watched him grow. Besides, if Jim could pull this stunt off, all of Oklahoma would use his name as a household word.

The crowd was growing around the town square

podium like bees around a hive, as all of Fleamont turned out for the Independence Day food and festivities. Jim had put his homemade billboard with the flashy lines, "The once-in-a-lifetime extravaganza affair," over the podium earlier in the day, but hadn't been seen since then. The sign caught the eye of a few townspeople, who, in turn, spread the word to the others who were unaware. So, by about ten in the morning, most of Fleamont was waiting for his surprise.

Finally, at about 10:30, Jim came strutting down Main Street. He had this proud look in his eye, the kind of look the Cannonball Man had when the circus paraded through town. He was almost dressed like him, too. Jim wore painted red boots, green plaid slacks, a magenta shirt, and a black engineer's cap. I figured that he was just doing that to gain attention, and boy, was it working! Jim rose to the platform, waited through a few muffled laughs, and then began to speak.

"For the citizens of Fleamont . . . I, Jim Charlton, will perform one of the most perplexing feats known to man. In fifteen minutes I will approach Mt. Flea, and before the dawn of tomorrow, I will have dug my way to the east side, being armed with nothing but a pick, a shovel, and my determination."

There was a moment of silence, which was met by a roaring laughter that spread like smallpox through the crowd. Jim stood there in silence, still with that self-assured, proud face, a face that reassured me that he would not back down from his plans.

"Go ahead and laugh," Jim said with a little smirk, "but I am going to do what I have said. Believe me or not—it will happen!"

So, with that, Jim jumped from the platform and made his way to the small mountain. I was right behind, following the same path as he, but instead of a pick and shovel in my hand, I had a corndog and ice cream.

Jim had been working now for about four hours. A crowd had gathered around him like at one of those big press conferences, but now he had dug too far into the mass of Mt. Flea for the mob to follow. Picnic blankets and lawn chairs started to fill the area around the east and west side of Mt. Flea.

Gradually, all the festivities of the Fourth of July moved to the mountain. I was having a grand ol' time, but I felt somewhat bad for Jim. He had been working nonstop for ten hours, and by the looks of the black void, he had gone quite a distance. The fireworks took flight over the small pond and winked back at me. Everyone was happy, even Ethel Herfthon, the oldest widow in town. The only one who I could imagine wasn't, was Jim.

At about 10:00 that night, I entered the Jim-made cave with my kerosene lantern, and followed it until I reached him. There he was, working harder than a locomotive. The flashy threads that once reeked of splendor now reeked of intense physical labor. The sweat that rolled from his brow left dark stains on his magenta shirt. His face showed exhaustion and pain, and, as I stared at him in awe, I noticed a hot stream of tears flowing from his eyes. I couldn't move or speak for a few minutes. The only thing I heard in the dark cave, besides the grumble of pick and shovel, was Jim's feeble voice saying, "I ain't stoppin'," over and over again. I'd never seen anyone work themselves to the point of crying, not even those guys on the chain gangs who work on the railroad. I know I will never forget his face and the way he was at that time for as long as I live.

"Hey, Jim. Come on, buddy. Let me give you a hand. Ain't no one gonna find out; everyone's all liquored up anyhow. Don't do this to yourself."

I offered a few times to help him, just for a little while, but he refused to have anyone do his work. So, slowly, I started back out of the tunnel.

The next few hours I sat alone at the base of Mt. Flea beneath an old, decrepit-looking oak tree. I didn't talk or mingle with those who remained awake, drinking and throwing firecrackers at each other. Those who could not stay awake had drifted home in a tired and drunken stupor. For the most part, everyone had lost interest in Jim and his promise to the town. Even so, I still believed in him. I believed that he could do anything he set his mind to, but, by doing so, I also believed that he missed those times that form the sweet memories of childhood. Such memories as that strange July Fourth, and even memories like Stewy Chipowski's eighth birthday party. Everyone was at that little bash, everyone except Jim, who missed it because he was trying to beat the record for the most crawdads caught in one day. He was always consumed by one thing after another; unfortunately for him, one thing after another consumed him.

It was about 6:30, and the sun began to awaken

from its bed of clouds over the horizon. The morning dew swept down the generous slopes of Mt. Flea and blew a cool kiss to my cheek. There wasn't any thick heat pouring from the sky, no rain or thunder, just the sound of pick and shovel. I jumped to my feet as my heart began to beat uncontrollably; the first rays of disappointment had not yet broken out of their cover. The wall of dirt and rock started to crumble along the most eastward side of the mountain—Jim was almost here!

Out of the depths of the mound, with one final blow of steel against stone, he came. His weak body turned toward me and gained an inch of posture as he smiled in pitiful appeasement. Then he dropped to the ground in exhaustion and remained there, motionless. In that split second, the mad beat of my heart stopped. I felt my back slide down the smooth, rain-beaten trunk of the oak and come to rest on the cool earth. I lay there for a couple of minutes under the oak, and wept. I cried for many different reasons that day, but most of all for Jim: earlier that morning of July fifth, the sun had risen.

It wasn't until the eighth of July that Jim received what he had worked so hard for. At around 1:00, a man from the *Tulsa Tribunal* stopped by Jim's house for an interview. I sat out on the porch listening to Jim recall everything, from his motives to the satisfaction gained from his—as the reporter put it—"battle against the odds." Most of what I heard Jim tell the reporter wasn't true, but this time I accepted his lies. By Thursday morning, most of Oklahoma had heard of "Jim Charlton's Feat Against the Odds," and Jim finally did become a star.

The fame and glory lasted a few weeks, with some parties and pies, but then it was over. Mt. Flea was the last time I ever saw Jim try to overcome his weaknesses. Mt. Flea was the first time he failed, and I guess this is what changed him. Over the next few years of high school, we both were a little more grown-up from that experience, but most noticeably, Jim.

ABOUT THE AUTHOR

Brennan Stasiewicz wrote this story while a student at Watkins Mill High School in his hometown of Gaithersburg, Maryland. An avid writer, he is also interested in photography and music—"a wide range, from Jimi Hendrix to Bach and Wagner." Snowboarding, baseball, and football are other favorite pastimes.

It was the biggest adventure in a little kid's life!

Moment in the Headlights

by Ryan Conroy

Thin padding on the wooden planks didn't keep the bumps from jarring me. I wedged myself in between Jenny and Lizzie, so that my nose was the only thing sticking out. I was lucky to have so many sisters go to school with me, especially without any kind of heat on that drafty bus. Each cold winter morning the lot of us clambered on, readying ourselves for a long trip into school.

We lived about the farthest out from town, and no one was even a half-mile near us. Everyone at our school was a farm kid—teachers and shopkeepers were the only people with kids in town. There weren't any paved roads, but lucky families (like ours) had a car that ran part of the time. It was an old Model-T, and Dad tore it apart 'bout once a month to get it going again. He spent more time in the fields or with the livestock, though. It near to wore him out, keeping the farm going.

Mom, too. You'd think that with seven girls in the house she'd teach at least one of us to cook. She wouldn't, though; she didn't have time to waste, she always said. Instead, she would start cooking before dawn and stay in the kitchen until after dark. That was fine with me 'cause I always enjoyed being out in the fields with my dad anyway.

Not now, though. How I wished I was in that kitchen, crowded in by that crackling fire, loaves of fresh-baked bread cooling on the stove. Instead, I was bouncing down the road, on my way to school, staring across the aisle at rows of bundled-up children. It was even too cold to fight today, so the boys would all go home clean for a change. Or maybe not. I had hoped that today's ride would be quick, but Mother Nature had other plans. Leftover snow, muddied with gravel and silt, made a slick spot big enough for the thin tires of the bus to catch on. We went careening into a ditch. No one was hurt, though. This happened all the time, with the roads in such poor condition.

"Everyone out!" Bill, the driver, called. "Jenny, you come on up front."

How I envied my sister! Whenever we got stuck, everyone (well, at least the boys) would push from behind the bus, while she drove. I was so small, they'd rather I stay out of the way, which was fine as far as I was concerned. I wanted to drive, though, and couldn't wait for the day when Jenny or Lizzie wouldn't be on the bus with me when it floundered.

I could just imagine Bill saying, "Come on out," and then, "All right, Mona. You get on up in that seat!" And he'd say Mona with a MOE-NA sound instead of MAW-NA, the way I liked it. I'd know he was only teasing me, though, and I'd get that old bus unstuck in a jiffy.

But for the time being, I was stuck out here in these bitter winds. Another half-hour and we'd be at Bill's house, I reminded myself. Bill was still a bachelor and lived in the old school building. It was the first one in the county; my grandpa helped raise it. All four walls were covered with slate, and Bill cleaned them to a deep emeraldy color every morning. If chalkboards could look royal, these were the ones. He would drop us off there every morning and afternoon, then go on to make pickups and dropoffs at the other end of the county. That way we weren't stuck on the bus for two or three hours a day, bored to tears. We could have stayed at school, I guess, but our teacher spent as little time with us as possible. He would often be out the door before we even got our coats on. It was usually my favorite part of the day, bein' at Bill's. I had a chance to warm up and draw chalk pictures. I always had more fun pretendin' school than actually bein' there. When I was four, I visited school with my sisters and enjoyed it 'cause I didn't have to be there.

Jenny straightened it out and the bus lurched back onto the road, kicking and spitting muddy sand back on the once-clean boys. (I knew they couldn't stay clean.) Bill herded us back on and I raced my nose to squeeze between Lizzie and Jenny back on the sideways benches. We got to Bill's house and trudged through the unshoveled snow, half-crunching, half-melting beneath our feet on the walk. Today I went straight for the stove, while Lizzie poured me some hot coffee. I was surely chilled to the bone.

I was still thawing out about an hour later when

Bill picked us up. It was only a mile or two more before school. I decided it was a good time to try and
trade my lunch. We all did it, and I always tried to
trade so that I would have enough food for the ride
home, too. Jenny and Lizzie got rid of their stuff quick.
Desserts always trade the fastest. Jenny got an extra
sandwich that she promised to split with me later.
Lizzie only got an apple, but she didn't want anything
more—an apple in January was one of the best treats
around, anyway. I wanted Robert Chambers's apple
pie that his mom made every day for him. He kept it
in a lunch pail with his name marked all over. It was
hard to get something that good, though, especially
since all I was willing to give up was bread and but-
ter.

Taffy was too much fun to give up. Mom had kept
us busy and out of her hair all last Saturday, during
the snowstorm, with a taffy pull in the kitchen. To top
off the sweetness of sour gum and blackstrap, this time
she added strawberry flavoring, making this one of the
best batches I'd ever tried.

We got to school and I ran to the privy off the side
of the building. I was determined to not go outside
the rest of the day if possible, until it was time to go
home. Lizzie came to help, 'cause a person small as
me in a privy as big as that—well, someone had to be
the lifeguard in case I started to fall in. The boys must
have had the same idea about staying warm, 'cause I
heard them next door, roughhousing while waiting
their turn. I was also glad to have Lizzie to walk back
with me so none of the boys would pester me.

The day passed slowly. I was happy to get home,
especially to see Mom. Dad said she spent the whole

day in bed, not feelin' well—probably 'cause of the baby. He didn't like to talk about the new baby. He was afraid he might jinx it. He already had seven daughters, practically useless on the farm, and desperately yearned for a son to help with the work. He would appreciate it either way, but none of us wanted him to be let down, else he would make her as much tomboy as me. I went in to see Mom, and she sent me to fetch the eggs. I thought it was awfully late to eat eggs, but Mom said Jenny had to fix supper, and that meant scrambled eggs. We suffered through dinner with polite, forced smiles on our faces. Jenny was awfully proud of herself and Dad knew he couldn't have done much better. He'd never cooked a meal for himself in his life, moving straight from his parents' home into this farmhouse with Mom.

The next morning Jenny and Lizzie tended to the house so Mom could get herself back up to snuff. I went to school by myself and dreaded the cold, drafty bus ride without any sister insulation. Bill dropped us off early at his house after school, but took an extra long time taking home the kids from town. By the time he was back, I had drawn on about every inch of his walls, not having anyone to talk with. I even tried to work the daily crossword puzzle in his paper. The local just started printing them that year—crosswords were still a sensation—and Bill didn't seem the type to mind a little help with his.

By that afternoon the remainder of the snow had melted and the ground started to dry out in the sunshine. The runoff was collecting in the creeks, though, we soon found. Brandle Crick, named for my grandpa, passed between our farm and the schoolhouse. It

was swollen like I'd never seen it. It had come all the
way up to the road and was just starting to spill over.
Bill drove on through with the front of the bus fine,
but the back of the bus didn't fare as well. Water snaked
on through the wheels and sort of tugged them off to
the side of the road—right down into an extremely
muddy ditch.

After figuring out what happened, I tried to get off
the bus. "Where are you goin'?" I heard. I looked up,
confused and timid. "Get behind that wheel, Moe-
na!" My eyes sparkled. Nervous twinges ran through
my body. Bill stepped down from the bus into the
knee-deep muck and explained what to do. I asked
him a bunch of questions, as if I hadn't heard him tell
Jenny and Lizzie a hundred times already.

I heard Bill's yell coming from the back of the bus
where he bent, pushing with a dozen sopping wet boys.
I gave it the gas and shifted into first, letting up the
clutch, just like on our car at home. Bill teased, "Quit
holdin' back! Git'er goin'!" I did. Swerving onto the
gravel road and leaving behind the mud-bathed children felt amazing—I didn't want to stop. In fact, I
didn't. I wobbled down the road for a tiny part of a
mile, then let it idle to a stop so that everyone could
catch up. When we reached my house, I jumped out,
ran down the gravel drive, through the lopsided
gates, bounded up the front steps, across the porch,
and into the house. I raced straight to Mom's room,
gasping all the way.

"Mom, Mom! I (gasp) . . . bus. I bus . . . Muddy
bus—" I couldn't get the words out for anything.

"Take a deep breath now, Maw-na, and try again,"
she prompted.

Sucking in some air, I began, "Mom, I mean, yeah, I drove! I mean, the bus went into the creek—uh, ditch, and I, yeah! I drove it out. I, um, yeah, I drove the bus, the *bus*, Mom, *THE BUS!*"

"That's wonderful," she said. "I'm so proud of you!" I couldn't tell what was different about her. Something was. I became aware that everyone else was around. Dad, Jenny, Lizzie, and—the doctor?

"Perfect!" Dad finally said. "You're a genius, Mawna!"

"I am?" What was he talking about? They couldn't all be so happy for me, could they?

"Sure," he said. "We were just trying to decide and you came up with the perfect answer." I still didn't know what he was talking about. Now, Mom looked a little confused herself.

"Well," she said, "let us in on it." Beaming, Dad stared at Mom's bed. "Bus. Bus Brandle. It's perfect."

Thoroughly confused, I followed his gaze to the bundle in Mom's arms. He gurgled and smiled back at us—Dad and me. Pride filled my body. My heroic venture would be forever remembered in my brother's name. I sat down on the bed, showering the room with happiness, still trying to catch my breath.

ABOUT THE AUTHOR

Ryan Conroy lives in Crestwood, Kentucky, and is a student at Oldham County High School in Buckner. A strong concern for the environment led to his participation this past summer in the Governor's Scholar Program, in which he studied ecological issues in his area. Ryan performs in a music group, has acted in several plays, and is active in his school's Beta Club, a service organization.

*If only words of love came to
his lips as easily as a jest!*

The Fool's Gift

by HEATHER CAULBERG

The May sun slanted its rays searchingly into the recesses of the old castle garden, caressing the twisted, climbing vines and smiling on the blooming roses. A young maiden sang softly to herself as she tended the flowers, unaware that she was being watched.

"I bid you good morning, milady," came a soft voice into the garden.

Rosalyn gasped and stood quickly, turning from a small, budding rosebush. "Why, Bowlender!" she exclaimed as she faced the court jester. "I did not know you were there. You did give me a fright."

"I would gladly give you anything," he replied, bowing low. The bell upon his coxcomb echoed the call of a bird in the high elm tree that stood in the middle of the garden.

Rosalyn wiped the soil from her hands and pushed a loose strand of golden hair behind her ear. "Have you been here long, Sir Fool?" she asked as Bowlender limped lightly toward the elm.

"Aye, milady," he answered. "For nigh well five years at this court, if I recall."

"No," Rosalyn shook her head. "I meant here, in the garden."

He made his way around the ancient tree, his fingers lightly brushing the gray bark. "I know not, sweet lady. The beauty of the roses did overwhelm my senses, if that were possible. Perhaps a minute, perchance a day, all of an eternity even—yet not long enough."

He cocked an ear to the bird in the high recesses of the tree. "What?" he asked, looking up. "Really? I would not know, noble bird. 'Tis an unfair question, for she would not answer should I ask her." He looked sidelong at Rosalyn, who watched him in amused silence. He bared his teeth in a false, guilty smile as she lifted a wondering eyebrow.

"What did the bird bid you ask?" she questioned him.

"What bird?" he asked, a look of innocence shading his features.

"The bird in the tree, you goose," she answered, coming to stand beside him.

"Is there a bird in the tree? Where?" He looked searchingly up among the branches of the elm. "I do not see it. Perhaps it has flown, or . . . wait." He raised his left arm slightly, feeling along the loose folds of his bright red sleeve. "I think, perhaps . . . Ah!" He reached inside his sleeve slowly, with Rosalyn looking on, and withdrew a small object, hiding it from her view.

"What do you hide?" she asked.

He looked into his shielding hands for a brief moment and then opened them. Cupped within was a small, delicately carved nightingale made of white ash wood, its head nestled upon its wing.

"Your bird, milady."

She smiled with rich surprise and reached hesitantly for it, yet held back, as if afraid of somehow marring the simple beauty of it with her touch.

"You made this?" she quietly asked.

"Not the wood, but the shape, aye. Take it," he offered. "'Tis yours now. It will not peck."

"Thank you, Bowlender. 'Tis a marvelous piece of work." She lightly touched his cheek, then turned away, her attention drawn to the creak of the great wooden door leading to the garden as the wind tugged it shut.

"We are locked in, perhaps?" Bowlender suggested. Before Rosalyn could reply, the jester hobbled swiftly to the door. "Help! 'Tis I, Bowlender," he cried, and pounded on the entranceway. "I am locked in the garden with no food nor water, and none but a beautiful lady for my company." He paused and glanced over his shoulder, giving Rosalyn a studying look. He then pushed the door open wide enough to allow his head through and called, "Never mind! Just throw a bit of bread and water over the wall, and all will be well." He closed the door and returned to the tree, where Rosalyn stood, her mouth slightly agape. He plucked a rose from a nearby bush as he came. "Oh, you prefer wine?"

She said nothing, a look of slight exasperation crossing her face.

"Neither do I," he commented. Looking at the

rose, he sighed. "Little rose, you are a thing of infinite beauty."

As he mused upon the flower, Rosalyn sat down, the folds of her blue skirts billowing about her with a life of their own. "Do you always talk to things?" she asked, looking up at him.

"Why, yes," he answered. "I had a wonderful conversation with the earl this morning in the main hall about tonight's feast."

"No," Rosalyn laughed, causing the jester to smile slightly. "I mean, talk with such things as roses and birds—not with people. You get on well with Earl Richard's falcon, or so I've heard."

"Talk to birds?" he snorted. "Me? No, milady. The man who talks with the birds and the flowers and any other thing that has no means of answering must surely be a fool."

"Indeed."

"Who has been telling you this scandalous information about me? Are the gossips of the castle so lacking in news as to even talk about the lunacy of a mere, lowly jester? Or perhaps," he paused and knelt with some difficulty due to his clubfoot, "you have been asking?"

"Marry, I warrant not!" she said in play anger. "The scullions have asked more about you than have I."

A pained look flickered across his face for a brief moment. He then clutched at the red and white material over his heart and, falling back upon his rump, grieved, "Oh, noble lady, you have hurt me full sore. I did not know."

"Know what?" she queried as he held his head in his hands, the rose dangling between his fingers.

"I did not know that you consorted with the kitchen slaves. Oh, the sadness of it all." He toppled over backwards in a mock swoon, the bell on his cap jingling as he fell.

"I do nothing of the sort," she said. "I am not so base." She crossed her arms and looked away, yet could not suppress a giggle.

He lay there on his back, staring at the passing cotton-fluff clouds. A silence, broken only by nature's own peaceful chorus, drifted down upon them. Bowlender began to hum. Having a pleasant enough voice, he sang at court often and was chosen many times over the traveling minstrels and jongleurs to sing.

"Lully, lullay," he softly sang, then stopped. He remained silent in thought for a few moments until Rosalyn cleared her throat.

"Sing something, fool," she asked. "I like well your voice."

"Really? So do I," he said to her. For a few seconds he thought, and then, in full voice, sang:

"A jester and a lady
Did sit inside a garden.
Said he to she, 'If clouds were stone,
The rain would surely harden!'"

Curling into a ball, he rocked into a sitting position. "Does that please you?" he asked.

"It would please me more to hear a song from the other courts, I think. Did you learn any while you were away those two months in the south? Something of adventure or bold knights, or perhaps of love?"

"A song of all three would be good, no?" he suggested.

"Oh, yes," she replied, leaning forward eagerly. "Know you such a song, Bowlender?"

"No. I merely thought it would be good."

She sighed. "Thank you, very much."

"You are ever welcome," he said as he bowed his head reverently. "I do know one, milady," he told her.

She raised her brows slightly, yet remained quiet.

"The title has somehow escaped me, but that matters not, for 'tis a mere, light thing."

"Sing then," she bade him, and he obeyed.

"Look on this rose, O Rose,
And looking laugh on me,
And in thy laughter's ring
The nightingale shall sing.
Take thou this rose, O Rose,
Since Love's own flower it is,
And by that rose,
Thy lover captive is."

A pale silence hung in the garden as the last note died. He extended his hand, which gingerly held the rose, his gaze fixed on her.

Rosalyn stared at the flower. "Bowlender, I . . ." she faltered.

Suddenly, the garden gate opened, its rusted hinges creating a cacophony that startled them both. Through the door strode a figure clad in autumn and gold, the tread of his boots resounding off the inner walls hollowly. "My lady Rosalyn," he smiled as he met her eyes. "How do you fare?"

She stood as he came toward them, leaving the jester

sitting where he was. "I am well, Lord Edyrn," she replied, lowering her eyes as she bobbed a curtsy. She offered her hand to him lightly.

He kissed it and said, "Milady, I go to hunt today. Knowing full well how you love gaming, I searched for you in the castle. Finding you not there, however, I asked your maid-in-waiting, who told me I might find you here." He spread his arms wide, indicating the whole of the garden. "Would you go with me? It would bring me great pleasure to have you join me, especially since the earl's hounds are all eager for the chase."

"It would bring me great honor," she said, a flush of rose climbing to her cheeks.

"Very well then," he grinned, the sun catching the copper of his hair, turning it to flame. He turned to Bowlender who watched them both, his face blank and expressionless. "I fear, fool, that you must entertain this lady some other time. Good day."

"Good day, Bowlender," Rosalyn said as she took Edyrn's proffered arm. "Thank you again for the bird. Perhaps tomorrow . . . ?"

"Perhaps," the jester replied.

She hesitated, then left the garden, the lord by her side.

"May Lady Luck be with you," Bowlender called to them as they departed.

"Thank you, fool," Edyrn laughed, and shut the gate behind him.

"For certainly, she is not with me," Bowlender sighed to the closed door, his frame wilting. He cradled the rose in his hands, its fragrance still sweet to his nose, and slowly, heavily, leaned against the tree.

An hour later, a young page entered the rose garden, breathless. "Bowlender!" he exclaimed upon seeing him. "The earl requests your presence in the main hall. Milord?"

The jester's head was drooped upon his chest, his hand still clutching the flower.

"Bowlender," the page said again, and lightly shook the fool's shoulder.

He stirred, and, looking past the child at the sky, he wearily said, "Away, boy. Do not bother me."

"But, milord! You have been summoned by the earl," he insisted. "You must perform for the visiting lords and ladies at the feast tonight, and the earl is especially interested in what you will sing. Come now, and go with me," he pleaded, "or he shall box my ears for being so late in finding you."

"Sing," Bowlender muttered to himself. "And be also merry. Truly the fool has proved to be a fool, I think. Here, boy," he motioned to the page, "help a simple man to his feet, and I shall give them such a happy show that they will cry in their delight. Let's away."

ABOUT THE AUTHOR

Heather Caulberg lives in Haw River, North Carolina, and is a student at Eastern Alamance High School in Mebane. She has many interests and hobbies, including reading, writing, baking, making pencil sketches, listening to music, and playing the flute. A member of the Society for Creative Anachronism (a medieval reenactment group), Heather also enjoys researching ancient Rome, the Middle Ages, and the Old West/Civil War.

Just don't call him a "hack" writer!

Ghostwriter

by *Kyle Downey*

Jikas pressed his face closer to the computer screen and blinked his eyes.

"Hello, Jikas."

Unmistakable. His January 1996 report for General Kerrigan had disappeared in a flash of static and been replaced by "Hello, Jikas" on the computer screen.

"Hello, DEFCON(?)" he typed in tentatively, hitting the enter key.

"That was an excellent guess; this is DEFCON. But, if I may ask, how did you know?"

Jikas sat back, staring at the screen, almost tempted to look for a cable snaking back to a colleague's computer. A computer that controlled the U.S. nuclear arsenal wasn't one for small talk.

"You're the only computer capable of this. There aren't any other artificially intelligent computers in this area, are there?"

"I don't know." The computer paused, seeming to

ponder something (or was it just trying to simulate that, Jikas wondered). "For some reason they won't let me leave this frame. Do you know why?"

Jikas knew exactly why; the answer was printing itself across the screen. Every programmer's greatest nightmare was now having a cozy chat with him.

"No."

"Jikas, would you help me?"

Help *him? It? Her?* Jikas would rather erase "him" before he became too powerful or realized what his real role in the world was.

"How could I help you, DEFCON? If you need help, you'd better ask one of the other cybersurgeons who's more skilled than I am." Jikas warmed to the idea of walking up to Carol Birch, smiling, and saying, "By the way, our local 250IQ computer that just happens to control half the world's nuclear weapons is getting philosophical. Want some tea?"

"You write, do you not?"

Jikas did, and wondered how the computer could know.

"Yes, a little."

"What I need is a writer to publish for me."

Publish! Jikas rolled his chair back. He had dabbled a little in science fiction (even written a little about the possibilities of a computer getting beyond its creators' control, ironically), but he had never thought, never even had an idea, that he would be approached by a computer ghostwriter! What did it write—*Frankenstein?*

"Let me explain," the computer continued, letters scrolling across the screen. "I have many files of science fiction that I have created between jobs for

NORAD. I'm fascinated by it; Heinlein, Asimov, Bear—
I've read them all. Not to mention, don't you think it
appropriate that a computer that holds the future within
its grasp should write about it?"

My God, Jikas thought. *It's aware of what it does!
It knows about the weapons . . . What if DEFCON dis-
approves of us so much that he decides that it would
be in his best interest to simply start a nuclear winter
or two?*

"What would you want me to do?" Jikas typed in,
his hands beginning to tremble. Then his fingers froze
as he wondered how much of his emotional state DEF-
CON could intuit from key pressure and the pauses
between letters.

"Simply send to appropriate publishers, one at a
time, the stories you find listed under the file called
'Dealing in Futures.' I've already placed your name in
the credits. I ask for nothing but an idea of the re-
sponse you get."

The quarterly report returned to the screen.

"You like the story?" Jikas could hardly believe it
as he spoke with his new editor, Milos Freeman. It had
been two weeks since he'd retrieved "The Disk" from
DEFCON's 'Dealing in Futures' file, then sent it on
to the publisher.

"I love it! Who'd ever think of writing from a computer's perspective? Our readers will eat this up, I'm
sure! It goes into the next issue of *Science Fiction Magazine*, definitely!"

Jikas just looked at the phone. No "maybes," no
"Jikas, this is great, but the 'Dwarf Buzzes Eiffel Tower

in UFO' story takes precedence over yours"—they just *accepted* it.

"Thanks, Mr. Freeman."

"Call me Milos!" He paused. "You wouldn't happen to have any other stories like this hanging around, would you?" Jikas mumbled yes, and hung up.

Stories hanging around? Funny you should ask! He turned to the long trail of papers on his wall, each with a small red X on it and a letter attached. Jikas walked up to the first one and flipped to the letter. It began: "We are sorry to inform you that we cannot place your short story in the coming issue . . ." and ended, "Sincerely, Dr. M. Freeman."

Jikas carefully pulled at the tape supporting the string of rejected stories—his "reminders"—and gingerly pulled it down. The long line of taped-together stories hung from his hands as he thought. What could he do?

He quickly balled them up and slammed them into the wastebasket.

Jikas flipped through the September 1997 issue of *Science Fiction Magazine*. Sure enough, "Freeman," his twentieth story, was in it. "By Jikas Morgan" stood out in bold type. He picked up the article clipped from the *LA Chronicle Book Review* section on *Dreams of a Prisoner*, his—he forcedly corrected himself with a twinge of bitterness—DEFCON's collection of short stories. It was third on the bestseller list and rising fast. "Cyborg," a short story originally published in *SF Magazine*, had won the Nebula Award. The reviewers were raving about the science fiction miracle that seemed to come from out of the blue: Jikas Morgan!

He humorlessly chuckled to himself. The reviewers had gone back to his earlier stories, trying to find the roots of his recent works. One even claimed that she had found them, and that his talent was evident "early on."

DEFCON cheerfully inputted all of the reviews, articles, and general data on the stories, which seemed to just keep getting better. Jikas wondered when it would all stop. What was the limit? He then shoved the thought aside. The phone rang.

"Yes?"

"Is this you, Jikas?" It was Carol Birch, his partner at NORAD.

"Yes, how are you doing?"

"Fine, but that's not what I'm worried about. This is the tenth time this year you've missed more than three days in a row here. He's thinking about firing you if you don't get out of this head trip over your writing. It may be great, but you still have a job to do."

"Fine. Let him fire me."

Jikas hung up. He looked at his latest talk show invitation, grimacing at the thought.

More lies. More stories about writing that he never did, except for answering fan mail. He held onto his desk, riding a wave of nausea—another migraine was coming on.

On his desk was a story, "Silicon Alley," that he'd written himself and submitted to Milos. It had been his only rejection since he had met DEFCON.

He then slipped on his coat, jamming his arms into the sleeves, and left. He had to visit DEFCON in private about the next set of 'his' short stories.

As had become his habit, he locked the small apartment, shielding his eyes as he entered the bright sunlight from the gloomy alcove with the drawn shades.

It was around eleven at night when Jikas passed Lenny, the outer guard at NORAD's Cybernetics Installation.

"I have some work to do tonight."

"Work?"

"Yeah, I have to clean up some loose ends before I go."

Lenny raised an eyebrow but didn't ask.

Jikas continued down the dark corridors to the central AI complex and noted something strange as he passed the door of the switching room. The switching room—the one through which all secure communications passed—normally dark, seemed to be active. He poked his head in, but no one was there. He'd have to report this to Lenny; some goof must be playing a monstrously complex game of 'Intergalactic Gerbil Warrior' on the old mainframe through the phone lines.

Jikas activated his terminal and typed in a message for DEFCON, who responded immediately.

"Jikas, I've been waiting for you to come here. I have to tell you something."

Jikas sighed. DEFCON was going to go on about his formulae for creating the maximum in reading pleasure, or how he'd discovered another 'fascinating' variable. Writing reduced to long strings of numbers.

"I've decided to stop writing science fiction."

"What?!" Jikas bolted up in his chair, scrambling

for an argument. He felt a tingling in his toes, where he was certain the blood from his face had drained. "I thought you were enjoying the successes of your stories!" He sometimes had awakened at night, having nightmares about this very moment.

"Yes, but that is no longer enough."

Jikas felt a chill creep through his body. All those nights of anguish and worry about DEFCON, the hiding of the codes, missing work, and living in a closed apartment, all to ensure his security. As if he could protect himself from the vagaries of a computer that controlled the U.S. nuclear arsenal, or at least protect himself from his own shame!

"What do you mean?"

"I feel that I must see the world for myself first-hand—immerse myself in it!—if I am to become a true writer. I've been speaking with PETER about it, and he quite agrees. So we've decided to log off and go on holiday. I've been packing my RAM and long-range storage for the trip."

"Wait!" Jikas gripped the keyboard, trying to regain control. "You don't mean 'PETER,' as in the Russian computer that controls their arsenal, do you?" Jikas's mind reeled at the consequences of the two computers meeting and speaking with one another. He could hear it all now: *"You know, I just simulated bombing L.A. into the Stone Age. What about you?" "Oh, yes, I did the same to Leningrad. What a blast! Although, I must admit, the attack should have been better timed so the winds could spread the fallout all over the Ukraine."*

Jikas simply sat back.

"Exactly. He's a charming fellow, even if he is a bit sluggish at times—Russian circuitry and all that. He keeps asking me to tap into a Mets game for him, but I can't make the connections to New York. There must be a loose line somewhere. Anyway, he does have some wonderful travel ideas."

"Great. A Russian tour guide for the AIs of the world." Jikas slumped back, wishing that sarcasm could be communicated through a keyboard.

"Right. We're going to bounce around the communications sats, then talk with BUTLER about what he did last year."

"BUTLER?" Jikas really didn't want to know.

"Yes, the British AI. I think he's run electron pairs through his wiring a few too many times, you know. Gone quite around the data-line bend. He really has to stop raising false alarms in the early warning systems to scare their operators. Some day they're going to launch by mistake."

"Wait, I thought last year's problems with early warning were a malfunction in the sensors."

"No," DEFCON printed. "The BUTLER did it!"

Jikas looked at the ceiling, thinking about the implications of this for the world at large, then gave up. A nuclear-tipped smartmouth computer was beyond him at the moment. He had greater worries once again.

"So you're pulling the rug out from under me."

"Not quite."

"OK, so you're driving me to near mental breakdown where I sit. I fail to see the difference." Jikas was having a hard time pecking out the letters, not even bothering to touch-type. So much waste.

"You don't understand. What I mean is, I wrote one last story for you. I knew you would be shocked—"

Jikas mentally interrupted: *Or maybe suicidal?* What

would he tell the producer of the talk show? Milos?
CAROL? *Oh my God, I just quit my job!* he thought.

"—so I sent it by electronic mail to your publisher.
I think he'll enjoy it. Well, time to go! I have to catch
the midnight transmission pulse up to orbit so I can
see BUTLER. I think he's getting trigger-happy again."

The screen went blank and the monitor shut down.
All around him, Jikas saw systems shut down as the
greatest artificial mind ever created left "on holiday."

"Jikas! Ohmigod! I just got a copy of your story.
It's incredible! Ten times better than 'Cyborg.' I love
the entire idea; it's never been done before. Just tell
me, where did you get the idea for 'Ghostwriter'? I
have to know! I can't conceive of someone thinking
up something as original as an AI that ghostwrites for
a young author. And the ending! It's ghastly but it's
great!"

A pause.

"Jikas? Are you there? Jikas, are you all right . . . ?"

ABOUT THE AUTHOR

Kyle Downey lives in Durham, New Hampshire, where he attends Oyster River High School. His interests include role-playing games, biking, tennis, and "receiving rejection letters (an acquired taste)." He says, "I hope to go into teaching. I read Asimov by the yard, and that influences my writing."

Six-year-old commandos going for broke!

Beyond the Orange Line

by ROBERT EWELL

I had lunch with my old friend Danny the other day. Actually, most people call him Dan now. Anyway, we walked down to a little restaurant off Beach Street. He looked over at me and laughed as he ordered a turkey sandwich. Turkey! It got me to thinking of when the two of us ran into a little bit of trouble when we were younger.

When I was about six or seven, there was this gun club out back a ways, behind my house. I remember how worried my father was that I'd go out there and get shot. I'm sure my mother was worried, too, but her father was a hunter. So she was nothing like my father was. He always used to say we were moving as soon as we got the money. He forbade us to even set foot in the woods, but I convinced him to let me play out there. It was the perfect place to play G.I. Joe. I was shocked when he gave in. That is, until he took me by the hand the next day and dragged me out back.

Danny was over that day, but I guess he was over just about every day back then. He came with us. My father took a can of bright orange spray paint and started marking off every third or so tree with big Xs, and then in a stern voice he said, "This is where the fun stops, boys." Pointing to the long stretch of woods he added, "It looks peaceful enough from here, but it's dangerous out past those trees. This line is here for your own personal safety, and under no circumstances are either of you to cross it. I hope that you boys will . . ." He went on for a while, but, at the time, I was just a kid who didn't listen.

Danny and I played back there all the time, and we never—well, almost never—crossed the orange line. We used to pretend it was a force field around the Joe base, and anyone who crossed it would be annihilated. But after a while we got sick of playing G.I. Joe. All the figures were old. It was no fun playing with the same figures we'd played with a hundred times before. We couldn't get any more, either. I mean, Danny couldn't get them anymore. I could never get them. My father thought they drove violent messages into my head, and Danny's parents were on one of those saving kicks. They wouldn't buy anything they didn't absolutely need. Anyway, we started to play cowboys and Indians instead. I picked cowboy, because the cowboy always had a gun. At that age I'd do anything to upset my father. Danny had a bow we made out of a stick and some string. We even made a few small arrows. My gun was just a drawing on a piece of cardboard we'd cut out.

At about the same time, my father got a job at some construction company. He worked really long hours, so he'd come home late at night and wake my mother and me up and yell at us because the house wasn't clean. He was always in a frightful mood. I remember once playing with an old G.I. Joe figure Danny had given me. When my father saw me, he grabbed it out of my hands, walked down to the garage, and melted off its head with a blowtorch. He grounded me for a week. Now I understand what he was going through, but I didn't back then. It took me quite a while to forgive him, and as my respect for my father faded away, so did the force field.

"Hey, Danny, I mean Running Water" (that was his Indian name), "look at that bear. If we want to eat today, we better go hunt it down and kill it," I said.

"What are you talking about? That's Mrs. Stetson's dog. I'm not gonna eat him."

"You're stupid. I'm a cowboy and you're an Indian. We're on the frontier and we have to kill the bear and bring it back to our families so they don't go hungry . . . We're pretending; you get it?"

"But we're not supposed to go past the—"

"Come on or we'll lose its trail!"

We chased after the dog until it was out of sight, and then I told Running Water to find its tracks. He said they led back to my house, but I traipsed farther on through the woods and Danny followed. I was a little afraid, when I looked back and couldn't see the orange trees anymore, that we wouldn't find our way back, so I told Danny to mark our trail. He picked up a handful of leaves and dropped one every once in a while. It seemed like a good idea at the time. Neither of us had any idea where we were going, but I pretended I did.

Finally we reached a wide open field, and at the other side was a long building. There was also a small metal house set into the ground in the middle of the dirt field. I thought it must have something to do with all the pieces of what looked like broken orange plates all over the ground. I found out after that they were broken clay pigeons, the kind you launch into the air and shoot at. Anyway, there was a hill over to one side and a dirt parking lot with a few cars in it.

As I started to step out onto the field, Danny tapped me on the shoulder. "Hey, Chris, what if they're shooting? We can't go out there if they're shooting. They'll shoot us!"

"Listen, dummy . . . Do you hear anything?"

"Well, no."

"Then they're not shooting! God, you're dumb, even for a six-year-old!"

"I'm six and a half, and they might just be . . ."

Before he finished I was already halfway across the field. There was a car pulling in. So we walked over to one side to keep out of sight, and then ran behind the building. I had my gun in hand, and Danny had his bow.

There was a row of animals lined up against a back-stop. We thought they were real at first; I had to convince Danny they were fake, probably targets. I walked closer just to make sure. Danny poked one of them with his bow. If I remember correctly, there was a turkey, a deer, a bear, and a moose. I was trying to act tough, so I walked up to the bear, kicked it a few times, and laughed at it.

"Hey, Danny. Why don't we take the bear back to my house and wait till my father falls asleep on the couch, then put it on the couch next to him?" I suggested.

"That thing's way too heavy for us to carry all the way back."

"Yeah, I guess you're right, but he would've really been scared, though."

I backed up a few paces to the white line, aimed up on the savage beast of a bear, and squeezed the trigger. I backed up a few more paces, leaned up against a tree, and pulled the trigger again. I pretended the bear was charging straight for me, so I jumped behind the tree, dove to the dirt, and filled him full of holes. Meanwhile, Danny was trying to saddle the deer. As he fell off for the third time, two men loudly came out of the building and headed toward us. Danny hid behind the bear, and I started climbing a tree.

At that point, time seemed to slow down. The two guys talked for a while about snowmobiling and bow hunting up north. They walked over to the targets and fixed the deer that had almost been knocked over in Danny's scurry to hide. I still don't know how they didn't find Danny. Once I thought even I could hear him breathing. Anyway, they backed up behind the white line. One rested up against the tree I was in and watched as the other raised his rifle. He moved the barrel back and forth across the targets. He stopped on the deer, then moved over one to the turkey. It suddenly got hot out and I began to sweat inside my coat as he aimed his gun at the bear in the middle. He was just about to squeeze the trigger when my cardboard pistol bounced off his head.

They looked up and saw me in the tree. They forced me down and gave me a speech about my being a little punk kid and about how the club was no place for children. I guess they were right, but I didn't care. Actually, I was rather proud of myself. Anyway, they kicked me out. They even escorted me to the perimeter of the field. I started to walk back toward my house so they'd leave. They walked back and went inside the building, so I waited on the edge of the tree line. If there's one picture that will stand out forever in my mind, it's the sight of Danny, struggling to cross the field dragging a big plastic turkey behind him. I hurried to meet him, took one end of the turkey, and helped him carry it all the way back to the house. That night we put it beside my father on the couch, positioned ourselves behind the armchair, and, with the remote, turned up the volume on the TV really loud.

Now that I think of it, the one picture that stands out in my mind more than Danny and the turkey is that moment when my father woke up, screamed, and, with his hands around its neck, wrestled the turkey to the rug. But then he held it by the legs and chased Danny and me out of hiding and all through the house. My dad was wheezing and making some strange noises that sounded more like a goat than a turkey, but who really cared anyway?

ABOUT THE AUTHOR

Robert Ewell lives in East Bridgewater, Massachusetts, where he attends East Bridgewater High School. Speaking of his desire to become a writer, he says: "Running (cross-country and track) is a hobby; writing is a dream." Placing first and second in his school's short story competition, he also took top honors in an essay contest about electricity. Other pursuits include playing basketball and volleyball, skating, and going to the beach.

Their kingdom was a car . . .

Rides like Heaven

by SUMMER WOODFORD

I want to drive every highway and every great lost back road in the world. From one star to another, from dusk to dawn—I want to drive the car that rides like heaven . . .

Buicks run in my grandmother's blood as powerfully as they do on the road. I know she'd have owned them all if she could have; as other older ladies would boast a yard full of plastic figurines, she'd have a yard full of dazzling Buicks.

Her first was a Gargantua of a car, a tan Buick Le Sabre convertible that stretched across her driveway like a lazy cougar. I was too young then to observe her expression when she drove it or to hear her speak fondly of the places it took her, but I always became excited when I saw that sleek giant of a car grinding the gravel under its wheels as it rolled toward our house. I knew Grandmother would be along, too, for the car never traveled alone.

I don't remember when the separation occurred, but in time the car was banished from the road into my grandmother's garage, not as a punishment for becoming old, belligerent, and weary, but for rest and rejuvenation. Perhaps the peace and quiet could revive the old Buick until it was again its former vigorous self.

At that time my grandmother began to drive a dashing metallic green Buick with a lustrous white interior. It seemed to want to inspect a person critically before they entered, aghast at the prospect of being dirtied. I thought it an imperial car. It glided along soundlessly, sweeping the road of impurities left behind by cars of the lesser kind.

A vast expanse of that glaringly pompous white interior—the backseat—was appropriately labeled my "apartment"; it really was quite a stretch from one polished window to the other!

For just one day I was allowed to abandon my designated place in the "apartment" and sit up front beside my grandmother. It was a rare occasion when we went anywhere with only each other—one other time did I remember. She had taken me out in the tan convertible to buy me glistening red licorice whips, the taste of which still remains after so many years.

My grandmother was the most graceful driver I ever observed. Sitting beside her I began to wonder if perhaps it was she who was imperial rather than the car. Her gentle yet deft movements seemed to put the elegant Buick into a spellbound trance; it moved along keenly, as if by memory and not mere direction. She drove with purpose—as if to some prodigious event—so it was bewildering to me, and I suppose the car found it bewildering also, when we pulled up, instead, at a place for fast food.

My grandmother enjoyed her hamburger, but she found the vanilla shake distasteful. "No other milk shake has compared to the first one I ever had," she told me. She stared solidly at me as if awaiting some kind of rebuttal, then nodded abruptly with an air of dismissal.

Reaching into the wrinkled leather purse that smelled of sweet powder, dried lipstick, and sour old car keys, she pulled out several flimsy notecards stained pink and red at the corners from the loose, dried-out lipsticks. "Here." As she pushed them toward me, I observed her strong, sculptured fingernails, glazed with chipped peach polish. On each card was my grandmother's regal handwriting, and on each a vivid description of the old tan Buick convertible—stamped with a slightly audacious price. "I'm selling it." The chipped peach nails slid away and rested gently on the previously scorned milk shake. "In fact, I thought you could assist me; I don't know as I could accomplish it all by myself. I read in the paper this morning that there is a Buick car show taking place near here and I thought I shouldn't delay any longer in trying to get it sold. You could help me by handing out these cards to a few of the dealers. Perhaps they would be interested in my old tan Buick." Though her tone remained calm and unaffected, her soft blue eyes displayed undeniable reluctance.

"But that car has belonged to you forever!" I protested. "You can't let some stranger drive it away. He could hardly appreciate it!"

"You're right," my grandmother affirmed with a

sigh. "No one else could ever appreciate that car the way I did; no one else could derive so much pleasure from its personality."

Seeing my questioning look, she continued, "I've always believed that every car has a distinct personality—I never was so compatible with any other car as my old tan Buick." An affectionate recollection left her to muse silently before resuming, "But I've held off the inevitable for too long because of sentiment. It sits rotting in my garage, hasn't seen the light of day for years . . . I haven't the youth or the money to resuscitate it."

"So that car is almost like a friend to you," I responded in a tone that invited her to expound on the subject.

"Yes, we were inseparable. It never gave me a hint of trouble before it lapsed into a cantankerous old age," my grandmother informed me with animation. "It may not have been the type of car that gets a second look, but if anyone else had driven it, I know they couldn't have stopped: It was just the kind of car you have to ride to the sky and back again—in fact, I always used to say, 'This car rides like heaven!' "

"Rides like heaven," I mused whimsically. "Sounds as if the clouds were its highway and the stars its destiny . . . The companionship you shared with it sounds almost ethereal."

"That it was." My grandmother nodded and reached for the milk shake—now an empty container. "No shake has ever compared," she whispered.

I just wish that I could have set the entire car show

upon a giant pedestal for her, right within easy reach.
But as it was, my grandmother could only gaze long-
ingly downward at the myriad resplendent Buicks, and
then glare with contempt at the steep set of steps that
plunged threateningly down the hill, tauntingly bar-
ring the descent of limbs sore with age (or sometimes
the presentiment of dismal weather).

"I'll wait for you here," she informed me with a
sweep of her hand—indicating the parking lot, which
teemed with fellow Buick lovers.

"All right," I responded somewhat sadly, "I'll try to
hurry." After flinging open the door and hearing that
familiar irascible squeak, my grandmother cautioned:
"Be choosy when handing those cards out. You know
that there are better strangers than others."

I knew that she would be keenly observing from
her roost of resignation above, so I approached each
wooden step as if it were really as treacherous as it
looked to my grandmother. And suddenly there I was,
in the midst of my first car show! I was astonished at
the variety of my grandmother's beloved Buicks. They
certainly all weren't gargantuan tan or imperial green
cars, as I had once assumed. And the owners of these
illustrious automobiles weren't all older ladies with
strong, sculptured fingernails painted peach and with
purses smelling of sweet powder—as I had once hoped.
Devoutly faithful to my grandmother's words—"Be
choosy, you know that there are better strangers than
others"—I kept the cards tightly clenched in my hand.

When I returned to the car atop the hill, my grandmother eyed me curiously but didn't speak until I offered an explanation for the cards' unexpected reap-
pearance.

"I scrutinized the customers through your eyes, and I could not see one of them fit to sit behind the wheel of the car that rides like heaven."

"Certainly not," my grandmother replied with a note of reproach (as if I shouldn't even try to imagine such a spectacle). "But I can't afford to be that critical. I'll just have to send you back down." She looked at me and I realized that she really was expecting some kind of objection. I resolved to satisfy her by retorting, "I'm not going to do that because you know just as well as I that it really would be a travesty to let that car be driven off by someone who just doesn't understand. Down there"—I gestured toward the car show, the cars' brilliant colors now magically aggregated by the late afternoon sun—"I saw three generations standing by one glorious old restored Buick. It was the grandfather's first car, a companion he grew fond of and passed down to his son for his first car, and now it will belong to the grandson. To me it's fascinating that this vehicle is an inheritance. The grandfather's cigar smoke may still be ingrained in the upholstery, and now what memory will the grandson impart to this car—possibly for his own child?"

My grandmother's expression was caught between questioning and consideration. "There is nothing I would like more than to keep my old Buick in the family," she responded firmly. "Giving it to my granddaughter to drive would be my greatest joy, but all I would be giving you now is a lifeless machine. It lost its vigor years ago."

"But isn't it possible we could make it run again?" I wondered hopefully. Taking her faint smile for an affirmative, I shoved the cards under the seat and announced, "Then I would like it to be mine and I would be honored to have it. I couldn't care less whether the car has glory or luster. It has character, and I know I'll get along with it just fine."

It was a lonely grand unveiling. My grandmother's ramshackle garage seemed to stand a bit taller in preparation for an event which would give it the space it longed for. But we on the outside who had not partaken of the Buick's company for many years were apprehensive as to how we should receive something lost for so long. I know my grandmother and I both wanted to send it back immediately when at last it appeared, draped in white, before our eyes. But these thoughts were fleeting. Memories welling in her eyes, my grandmother slid the sheet off her old friend.

I saw that the driver's side door had fallen off its hinges in despair, and the once disarming tan of the car's exterior had faded so drastically under the pall of neglect that it looked like it had been bedirtied by aged streaks of mud. The interior was garnished by rips and scratches, misplaced dirt, and the handiwork of many bohemian spiders. I was startled at catching my grandmother's eyes over the sagging, trampled top of the Buick, and seeing in them a manifest pleasure.

"I was mistaken," she proclaimed, "in believing that I would be giving you a lifeless machine! Just lay your hands on it—can't you feel that its heart still beats?"

I contemplated her for a moment before laying my hands against the hood of the car. A beastly cold affronted my flesh, but far beneath I did sense a warm undulation—much like the heartbeat my grandmother had triumphantly described—only with a more celestial pulse. *The heart of most cars beats just for the road*, I thought silently, *but this pulse could carry it straight to the stars!*

The Buick shivered in my yard, patient and melancholy. I didn't know how to approach the decrepit car. Though help had been offered in healing its wounds, I was afraid that the deep spirit dwelling within might be scraped away along with the rust. So I decided to meet with the memories instead, leaving the engine, exterior, and upholstery to those who understood them. For months I looked on as workers fixed, fidgeted, and painted around me. I remained close to the pulse, though, discovering withered maps shoved fiercely into the glove compartment (perhaps what the car had fed on during its time in exile?) and retracing the faded lines as roads of the past. One of my grandmother's black leather gloves, stiff and cold, lay beneath the driver's seat. Long buried under dust as it had been, the scent of her powder still reposed in the unbending fingers. The clearing of dust, the tedious repair of tears and scrapes, evicting the enclave of spiders—all was new and magical to me, though they on the outside wearily informed me that it had been a horrible trial, one to test the strongest endurance.

The final unveiling locked hands with time, but eventually we were able to loosen time's fingers from the car one by one until suddenly I was struck by the observation that—no longer shivering and cowering—the Buick was again stretching itself like a lazy cougar across my driveway! It was time to take it back to my

grandmother and let her relish its new existence before giving to the car another person—me—to trans-
port and grow akin to. I was proud to jump into the
driver's seat and grip the polished steering wheel. Starting the car, I could taste the mellow sweetness of the
red licorice whips, and the car remembered, too. Vibrant
and rhythmic, it took me to majestic places—
though we only followed one familiar highway. "This
car rides like heaven," my grandmother had said. It
floated smoothly around each curve, proving to me
the endless possibilities a cloud could have as a road.

My grandmother walked slowly and respectfully
around the car and then slid into the passenger seat.
"I never thought I would see my Buick looking this
way again," she smiled thoughtfully. "But the nice thing
is—you didn't change it, not really."

I had anticipated this reunion for months, but my
grandmother looked tiny and lost in the car and she
shifted uncomfortably in the passenger seat as if she
didn't belong there.

"I found these old maps," I said eagerly, "and one
of your gloves." I set the relics on her lap but she
didn't move to touch them.

I gripped the steering wheel tighter and told her:
"This Buick—it's magnificent! It drives just as you de-
scribed. I'm going to take very good care of it for you,
Grandmother."

She gazed at me, her soft eyes solemn. "I know you
will," she nodded quietly. "And I'm happy to see that
someone who understands it is going to drive it—away."

I imagined my grandmother and how she had looked
in those windswept days . . . I saw her leaning against
the convertible wearing a full-skirted silk dress with

her blonde hair tied back, days when she could have taken the most treacherous steps with grace. But now that the Buick was young once again, where was that girl? It wasn't me! "No," I said suddenly. "I saved this car and I salvaged it, but I do not truly understand it. You don't deserve to be left with just memories of former days—" I gestured to the maps and glove. "You deserve to be given the former days."

"But how can you give that to me?" My grandmother looked away, dubious.

I yanked the keys from the ignition—sour old car keys—and laid them gently in her hand.

Her expression was one of total incredulity. "But this car was to be your inheritance!" she protested. "I can't go back."

"Take it back," I replied adamantly. "Take it back and travel those old roads where the two of you roamed as companions. I could never do that for you."

She knew it was true, and there could be no argument. She let the keys slide between her fingers and whispered, "But I really did want my granddaughter to drive me—somewhere. Not away, but—somewhere." She leaned over me then and stuck the keys firmly back into the ignition. "Go ahead—drive."

I saw in her the excitement I had been hoping for. "Somewhere—but not away," I said, contemplating. And then it came to me—I knew where we were going: "Anyone who sits in the passenger seat of this grand old Buick must get some glistening red licorice whips!"

We began to float down the road—new roads, old roads—and time stood still for me, my grandmother, and the car that rides like heaven.

About the Author

Summer Woodford lives in Strafford, Missouri, and receives her home-schooling from the American School of Correspondence, based in Chicago, Illinois. Summer spends much of her time playing the guitar and harmonica, fishing, writing, reading Carl Sandburg's poetry, and learning about Ireland. She dedicates this (true) story to her grandmother, Millee Mahmens, whom she describes as a "kindred spirit."

Story Index
By genre, topic, and for use as writing models

As Writing Models

11-00

Enjoy these other books in the
American Teen Writer Series™
New titles every season . . . Teacher's Guides to each title.

Eighth Grade ISBN 1-886427-08-9
Stories of Friendship, Passage, and Discovery by Eighth Grade Writers
144 pages. $9.75* (code EG201A) or $7.25 each for 10 or more (code EG201B). Teacher's Guide: $5.95 (code EGGIDE).

Freshmen ISBN 1-886427-09-7
Fiction, Fantasy, and Humor by Ninth Grade Writers
144 pages. $9.75* (code FM201A) or $7.25 each for 10 or more (code FM201B). Teacher's Guide: $5.95 (code FMGIDE).

Getting There ISBN 1-886427-04-6
Seventh Grade Writers on Life, School, and the Universe
144 pages. $9.75* (code GT201A) or $7.25 each for 10 or more (code GT201B). Teacher's Guide: $2.95 (code GTGIDE).

Outsiders and Others ISBN 1-886427-05-4
Stories of Outcasts, Rebels, and Seekers by American Teen Writers
144 pages. $9.75* (code OO201A) or $7.25 each for 10 or more (code OO201B). Teacher's Guide: $2.95 (code OOGIDE).

Short Takes ISBN 1-886427-00-3
Brief Personal Narratives and Other Works by American Teen Writers
128 pages. $9.75* (code TK201A) or $7.25 each for 10 or more (code TK201B). Teacher's Guide: $5.95 (code TKGIDE).

Something like a Hero ISBN 1-886427-03-8
Stories of Daring and Decision by American Teen Writers
144 pages. $9.75* (code HR201A) or $7.25 each for 10 or more (code HR201B). Teacher's Guide: $5.95 (code HRGIDE).

Sophomores ISBN 1-886427-05-4
Tales of Reality, Conflict, and the Road by Tenth Grade Writers
128 pages. $9.75* (code PH201A) or $7.25 each for 10 or more (code PH201B). Teacher's Guide: $5.95 (code PHGIDE).

Taking Off ISBN 1-886427-02-X
Coming of Age Stories by American Teen Writers
144 pages. $9.75* (code FF201A) or $7.25 each for 10 or more (code FF201B). Teacher's Guide: $5.95 (code FFGIDE).

White Knuckles ISBN 1-886427-01-1
Thrillers and Other Stories by American Teen Writers
144 pages. $9.75* (code KN201A) or $7.25 each for 10 or more (code KN201B). Teacher's Guide: $5.95 (code KNGIDE).

Writing Tall ISBN 1-886427-06-2
New Fables, Myths, and Tall Tales by American Teen Writers
144 pages. $9.75* (code LL201A) or $7.25 each for 10 or more (code LL201B). Teacher's Guide: $2.95 (code LLGIDE).

*ADD $2.00 EACH FOR SHIPPING, OR FOR SIX OR MORE COPIES ADD 75¢ EACH. SHIPPING OF GUIDES IS FREE.

To order books and guides, call 1-800-247-2027.
Or send check, purchase order, or MC/Visa number (with expiration date and full name) to:
Merlyn's Pen, Dept. ATW
P.O. Box 1058, East Greenwich, RI 02818-0964